CAULDRONS & CHARACTERS

A LIBRARY WITCH MYSTERY: BOOK 15

ELLE ADAMS

1

***

"Sylvester, can you please get off the tree?" I leaned over the balcony and shooed the owl away from the top of the towering Christmas tree that now dominated the lobby. It'd taken the better part of the morning to put the tree up, and we'd scarcely started the actual decorating before Sylvester had planted himself on top and began singing carols at full volume.

Preparing for Christmas in a magical library inevitably came with chaos as a built-in expectation, but I didn't recall the owl being this much of a nuisance last year. If anything, I'd assumed setting up the tree a few weeks early would dampen the excitement a bit. Sylvester had already eaten an entire roll of tinsel, which might have given me cause for concern if he'd been a real owl and not the embodiment of the library's entire store of knowledge. One would think that fact would mean he didn't need to bother himself with such mundane things as human holidays, but he never passed up an opportunity to claim his spot as the centre of attention.

"Sylvester, can't you go and help the visitors instead?" Estelle called up to him. My cousin stood at the bottom of the tree, holding the other end of the tinsel we were draping around its branches in one hand and her wand in the other. Curvy and tall like her mother, she shared the same red curly hair common to all our family members, and we wore the same silver-lined black cloaks embossed with the family's logo of an owl sitting atop a book beneath a pair of crossed wands.

"I did." He fluttered onto the balcony and spread out his tawny wings. "I sent them to the Dimensional Studies Section."

"You didn't, did you?" I never could tell whether the owl was joking or not. Nobody ever went into *that* section of the library voluntarily. It was the sort of place you fell into while trying to get somewhere else. "If you did, can you please get them out of there? We're busy."

"Allow me to solve that for you." Sylvester leaned over the balcony and grabbed the end of the tinsel in his mouth, tugging it loose from the tree.

"Sylvester!" I lifted my wand and cast a quick levitation charm, and the tinsel came to a halt in midair before it all went tumbling down onto Estelle's head. "What was that for?"

"Don't you want to help your visitors?" he enquired.

"You're the one who trapped them in there—if you aren't having me on." I levitated the tinsel back into its proper place. "I realise it's a bit early for Christmas decorations, but I thought we needed some holiday cheer after everything we've been through recently."

After the turmoil of the last few months, I would have expected even Sylvester to agree. In fairness, he didn't seem to find the holidays themselves objectionable, only our choice of décor. It also didn't help that Estelle and I had ended up handling most of it alone, as Aunt Adelaide was busy handing out textbooks to students cramming for end-of-term exams while Cass and Aunt Candace never volunteered themselves to help with anything most of the time. Jet, my crow familiar, did his part by flying around hanging up baubles alongside Spark, Estelle's pixie sidekick, while singing carols in squeaky voices. Unfortunately, neither of them was a match for Sylvester. He offered a loud cackle in answer.

"What's he done now?" Estelle called up to me.

"Supposedly he led some people to the Dimensional Studies Section," I replied. "I'll get them out. I'm closer than you are."

"Are you sure?" She frowned at Sylvester. "That's a bit much, even for you."

"It's a harmless prank," he retorted. "I thought you were trying to lighten the mood."

"That's not what I meant," she said. "Honestly. If you're sure, Rory. I'll wait here."

"Don't cause any more trouble while I'm gone," I warned the owl. As far as pranks went, it wasn't his worst, but the Dimensional Studies Section was disorientating at best, not to mention mildly traumatising for the unprepared. "I'll be right back."

I was already on the second-floor balcony, so it was a simple matter to climb the nearby staircase and track down the elusive area that was halfway between the second and third floors. With an interdimensional corridor, it was a tad difficult to pin down its exact location. When I stepped off the stairs, I found my feet planted on a carpet patterned with spirals that moved in time with my steps and made my head spin to look at. On either side stood a row of shifting bookshelves that also constantly moved, shifting sideways and up and down as if they were on some kind of multidimensional conveyer belt. Which wasn't that inaccurate. Needless to say, I'd never actually *read* any of the books in here. If the pages were as unpredictable as the shelves, it would be a headache and a half trying to make sense of their contents.

I found the unfortunate visitors—a pair of twenty-something witches maybe a year or so out of university—clinging to a ladder propped against the shelves to keep from being swept away by the sliding carpet. With each jolt of the shelves behind the ladder, they let out shrieks of alarm. I moved that way.

When the floor lurched sideways, I gave it a stern look. "Hey, stop that."

"Help us!" yelled one of the witches.

Really, Sylvester? I braced my feet, and the carpet mercifully came to a halt. After nearly a year in the library, I'd grown wise to some of its tricks, including this one.

"Hang on," I called to the witches. "I'll get you out of here."

The corridor responded with another sideways lurch that caused me to stumble, hands grabbing for the shelf to catch my balance before I fell into an undignified face-plant. "Whoa."

"You work here?" asked one of the witches, who had bottle-blond hair and the sort of pale complexion that I associated with people like my aunt Candace, who spent all her time indoors hunched over a desk. "Can you tell us where the secret corridor is?"

"The *what?*" I very nearly did lose my balance then. "You were looking for a secret corridor?"

"*The* secret corridor," said her equally pasty companion, who had a vibrant streak of pink in her dark hair. "We heard a rumour at the pub that you have a secret corridor containing a book that can grant your heart's desire."

"A book that can *what?*" I sounded like a broken record, but the words "secret corridor" put together with "heart's desire" set off a cascade of warning bells in my head. Nobody outside of the library was supposed to know the fourth-floor corridor existed, nor what it could achieve, and its cranky guardian enforced that rule with brutal efficiency. "Nope. Whoever told you that was lying. There's no such thing as a book that can grant your heart's desire. If there was, it wouldn't be such a huge secret, would it?"

Not my best diversion, but I'd been at least partially honest. The wish-granting didn't come from a book but from a hidden door in a corridor that had gone missing for decades until its recent rediscovery.

"I told you it was nonsense, Corrine." The first witch poked the second in the arm and then gave a shrill scream when the shelf lurched upward and carried the ladder with it.

Both witches were sent flying into the air, as though propelled from a trampoline, and I hastily lifted my wand and cast a levitation spell before they hit the ground. I could have used my Biblio-Witch Inventory instead, but that would require two hands, and I didn't quite dare let go of the shelf. They landed on the swirling carpet and held on to the nearby shelf for dear life.

Now that I knew what the pair of witches were looking for, I understood why Sylvester had sent them somewhere they wouldn't be able to cause trouble, but I could hardly leave them stuck in here all day. Being semi-sentient, the library itself reacted against people it didn't want probing into its secrets, but a pair of overly curious witches didn't deserve to face the wrath of the corridor's guardian.

"It *is* nonsense," I repeated, hoping the library would get the message and help me get them out before they could cause any more agitation. "I'm not going to pretend the library doesn't have hidden nooks and crannies since we're standing in one right now, but plainly there's nothing in here that can offer your heart's desire. Unless your desire is to go into the fifth dimension and never come out."

Okay, I'd made the last part up, but Sylvester had frequently claimed the Dimensional Studies Section did contain dimensions not visible to the human eye. While most of his claims were outright nonsense, some did hold a kernel of truth, and I'd learned not to cast limits on what a semi-sentient library was capable of.

"We just wanted to look!" squeaked Corrine. "Can you help us out of here? I promise we won't come back."

"I can try." I faced the shelves and spoke clearly to the library. "You can let them go now. They won't come up here again."

The library showed no signs of having heard me, but its communication style was obtuse at best. My grandmother had created the place to be semi-sentient, but since she'd died without leaving clear instructions—not to mention a map—we were still uncovering new secrets every week.

With a creak that sounded like a sigh, the shelves stopped their dizzying shuffle, and the ladder settled on the ground, letting the witches climb down. They took off at a run, and I followed closely behind as they emerged, gasping, onto the main staircase. Once I was sure they were going down to the lobby, I returned to the second floor. Sylvester remained perched on the balcony where I'd left him, a smug expression on his face.

"You might've mentioned they were trying to get into *that* corridor," I whispered to him. "I'd have got rid of them myself."

"Ah, but a visit to the Dimensional Studies Section leaves more of an impression, doesn't it?"

"All right, you win." I returned to the tree. "Let's get this tinsel sorted. Do you promise to behave, Sylvester?"

The owl shuffled his feathers in answer.

"Everything okay up there?" Estelle peered up at me from below with a questioning look on her face.

"Yeah—I'll explain later." Best to get this over with before Sylvester decided to wrap me in tinsel again, mummy style, as he'd done on our first attempt at decorating.

This time, we got off lightly, and he let Estelle and me finish draping the tinsel around the tree without doing much except stealing a few baubles.

"He's more of a magpie than an owl," Estelle remarked when she saw him soar out of sight. "I hope he doesn't try eating those."

"Don't give him ideas." At least we had no shortage of spares. The library was massive enough that it would take a week to decorate all three main floors. As well as smaller trees being put on each floor, the shelves would be topped with tinsel, holly would be entwined along the balconies and stairs, and fake snowflakes would drift gently over the lobby.

The fourth floor, however, would remain decoration free —and hopefully, free of overly curious visitors too. *Heard a rumour at the pub, did they?* My aunt Adelaide would certainly want to know about that one.

"All we need to do now is put the angel on top," Estelle said. "Ready?"

"Sure, I'll get it." I looked in the box and found a dead mouse in place of the angel. "Oh, charming. Sylvester?"

"Yes?" His tone was sugary enough to give me a toothache.

"Sylvester, did you steal the angel?"

The owl gave me an affronted look. "I stole nothing."

"Come on." I frowned at him. "What's the problem? You have free run—or flight—of the entire library. We're not encroaching on your space."

"I never said you were."

"Why steal the angel?" Estelle tilted her head. "Do you want us to put an owl on top of the tree instead? Is that it?"

I stifled a laugh. "That's it, isn't it? You hate not being the centre of attention."

The tree gave an alarming lurch sideways, shedding tinsel. I pointed my wand at it, hastily, one eye on Sylvester.

"I wasn't trying to make fun of you," I said quickly. "But you know, people kinda expect an angel to be on top of the tree. Or you can have your own tree instead?"

The tree stopped lurching, settling back into place in a clatter of baubles. "That *may* suffice."

"Can't the Forbidden Room conjure one up?" The room, which was the owl's true domain, made the Dimensional Studies Section look like a harmless cupboard in comparison. Its magic seemed to hold no bounds, and it operated under the simple rule that each of our family members got to ask one question per day and the owl would answer, generally with conditions. With that kind of power at his disposal, you'd think he'd be able to summon up a Christmas tree.

"Nobody ever asks what I want," he said with a wistful sigh.

"There's no need to be dramatic." *All right, fine.* It was a waste of a question, but since I got one per day and I didn't have anything else I wanted to ask for urgently today, using up my question was a small price to pay for the chance to decorate the real tree in peace. "If I do as you ask, will you put the angel back where it's supposed to be?"

"Consider it done."

"Good." I peered over the balcony. "Estelle, is the Book of Questions down there?"

"Should be. What does he want?"

"His own Christmas tree." Not covered in dead rodents, I hoped. I'd decided compromising was the best option, but that owl truly was perplexing sometimes. "He did me a favour when he got rid of those witches."

Probably he thought I owed him one in exchange too.

Estelle's brow wrinkled. "We have room for two, but we might have to do some rearranging."

"I'll figure it out." I made my way to the stairs, which curved all the way down to the ground floor. An identical staircase lay on the library's opposite side, stopping off at each of the library's three main floors and offering an impressive view of the shelves below. The ground floor also contained a number of large tables and classrooms for students to use for group projects and the ever-popular Reading Corner encased in the middle of the Fiction Section near the back. We'd planned to put the tree just to the left of the Reading Corner so that it was in full view of the library's most popular corner, but I'd have to ask Aunt Adelaide if she minded shunting it over to make room for another one. I'd also tell her about the two witches' unexpected visit while I was at it too.

The universe said otherwise. I was halfway to the first floor when a loud hissing noise came from above, sounding somewhere between a giant serpent and a gas leak. *What in the world was that?*

Estelle came running to the stairs. "What's going on?"

"No clue," I called down to her. "It sounded like an animal."

My other cousin's penchant for rescuing magical beasts and bringing them to the library was well known, but a giant snake was a new one. *Don't tell me she found a basilisk this time. Or a wyrm.*

"That's what I'm afraid of." Estelle hurried up two flights of stairs to join me, and we made our way upward to the library's topmost floor.

Well, *almost* at the top. The third floor was the location of both the Magical Creatures Division—where Cass spent the majority of her time looking after her array of magical pets— and the door to the once-missing fourth-floor corridor. A strange noise from either of those places was bad news, but a new magical monster was at least a vaguely known factor. My heart sank when another hissing noise filled the air, louder than the first.

"Was that the fourth floor?" Apparently so. "Please tell me Aunt Candace isn't trying to get through the doors again."

Most of the doors upstairs were locked even to our family members. The notable exception was a door that would grant us any wish we desired, once per day, like the Book of Questions. I wasn't sure who had come up with the idea first —Sylvester or my grandmother—and the owl had insinuated that I'd be better off avoiding that question if I wanted my eyeballs to stay where they were supposed to be.

Bracing myself, I crossed the third floor, ducking around shelves full of books covered in fur, feathers, and fangs. Some growled at me when I walked past, and others had escaped their shelves, as though scrambling to avoid whatever had made that hissing noise. While Estelle hastened to put them back into place, I spied Cass exiting the fourth-floor corridor, her red hair tied back in its usual messy bun and her glasses perched on the end of her nose. Willowy and tall like Aunt Candace, she always smelled faintly of animals —not that she'd appreciate me pointing that out.

"What's going on?" I asked her. "What were you doing up there? Not summoning a basilisk, I hope."

Please, no. Cass had been surprisingly disinterested in the corridor's wish-granting powers, but I knew that seeming lack of curiosity would only last until she took a fancy to a new magical monster that she couldn't obtain through any normal means.

"A basilisk?" Interest gleamed in her eyes. "No, but if I wanted one of those, I could just buy an egg."

"Please don't." Estelle caught up to me. "What's going on?"

Cass blew out a breath. "Yeah… Aunt Candace has a dead body up there."

"She has a *what?*"

Estelle and I exchanged alarmed looks. Had someone else trespassed upstairs? I'd thought the guardian wanted to *avoid* drawing attention to the library's secrets, and surely even Cass would have had more of a reaction if someone was actually dead.

Cass shrugged and stepped aside as I ran through the door, my pulse racing.

At the top of the stairs stood my aunt Candace. She and Cass shared the same tall willowy frame, except instead of drab colours, our aunt usually dressed in bright flowery dresses. The notebook and pen that usually floated at her side were conspicuously absent.

She also did indeed stand next to a body—or something that strongly resembled one. A broad-shouldered, dark-haired man lay face down on the floor outside the door to the wish-granting room, and while I could only see the back of his head, he didn't look familiar to me in the least.

"What did you *do?*" I asked Aunt Candace.

From the pen she held in her hand, I could only assume she'd written a wish on the door to the room, but why would it have given her a dead body in exchange? "Don't tell me you went too far while doing book research on the best ways to murder someone."

"He isn't dead," she said. "Well, not *that* dead anyway."

"He looks dead to me." Estelle peered at the back of his head. "Aunt Candace, who *is* he?"

"I'd have thought you'd recognise him," she said to her niece. "His name is Jaxon Hyde."

"What?" Estelle goggled at the man. "Jaxon Hyde? You mean from that paranormal romance series of yours?"

"He came from one of your books?" My attention jerked over to the open door to the wishing room. "Seriously?"

"Technically, he came from the small town of Moonfang Cliff."

Estelle groaned. "You conjured up one of your book characters?"

Surely, she hadn't intended for him to be dead when he showed up, and while a dead body in the library wasn't ideal, nobody here would know who he was. How would reporting a fictional dead body even work, without getting into the infinitely more tangled question of how real a character who'd come out of a book truly was?

"Why?" Judging by the man's casual clothing, he wasn't from one of her fantasy worlds where everyone walked around dressed in armour, but that didn't mean he would have been remotely equipped for *this* world if he'd come out of that room living and breathing. "Why him?"

"To revive my love life, of course," said Aunt Candace. "The real men in town are a disappointment, and I thought... well, the room's right here, isn't it?"

"You conjured up a book character to go on a date with?" She had to be joking. "You used the room's powerful magic on something as trivial as that?"

"Cass used the room to dispose of a large quantity of manticore dung the other day."

Lovely.

"That's not remotely the same," I said. "Would *he* get a say in whether he goes on a date with you or not?"

"Obviously," she said. "Granted, I'll have to come back tomorrow and ask the room to bring me a living version instead of a dead one, but this is progress, isn't it?"

"No," said Estelle. "You're going to put that man back right now and never try anything like this again."

"I can't," she said with a touch of smugness. "The door only opens once a day."

"For each of us," I corrected. "We each get one wish per day, which means one of us can get rid of him."

"Exactly." Estelle stepped in. "This is out of the question, Aunt Candace. You can't bring a fictional character to life, let alone a vampire."

"He's a vampire?" Wait a moment. If he was anything like the kind of vampires that existed in real life, moving and breathing weren't necessarily prerequisites for being alive—if the term even applied to vampires in the regular sense. "Are you sure he's—"

Aunt Candace grinned. "Now she gets it."

That was when the man stirred.

2

The vampire rose and let out a loud hiss that echoed down the corridor and caused all three of us to instinctively back away. *Oh,* I thought numbly. *That's what the noise was.*

Aunt Candace gave a squeal of delight. "I knew you were just stunned. Are you okay, Jaxon?"

The vampire stopped hissing and stared at my aunt in open bewilderment. "Do I know you?"

"Oh, you will," said Aunt Candace with a grin on her face that made me want to give her a thwack on the back of her head. "I'm Candace Hawthorn. Those clueless-looking youths behind you are my nieces, Estelle and Rory."

"How do you know my name?" The man's baffled expression seemed genuine enough that it made me wonder just how much he remembered of his former life before he'd been yanked into our universe. Did he even know he was a fictional character? "I don't remember meeting you before."

"You may have caught a touch of amnesia," she said. "You'll get over it."

She can't be serious. Admittedly, none of the rest of us had a better explanation, and instinct told me it was unwise to mention that Aunt Candace had literally *created* him.

"Where am I?" he asked. "What is this place?"

"The library," Aunt Candace said. "I'll show you around."

Both Estelle and I tried to catch her eye on the way past, but she ignored us, putting on a sunny smile as she beckoned Jaxon to follow her to the stairs. He moved with the same eerie grace as any vampire I'd met, though his fangs hadn't made an obvious appearance yet. Come to think of it, how many of the rules I was used to even applied to the vampires in Aunt Candace's novels? I'd never read the series he'd come from, and I had to wonder why she'd picked him above all other available options.

"She has got to be joking," I muttered to Estelle as the two disappeared downstairs. "What's her long-term plan with this? How long will that guy even stick around?"

"Not long, with any luck," she murmured back. "This isn't her first attempt to summon one of her characters, but I don't know why this one worked and the others didn't."

He's not the first character she's tried to conjure out of that room? I didn't quite know how the room's magic worked, but Grandma had intended for the corridor to be for our family alone and had created the guardian to enforce that rule. While I saw no signs of the ghostly security guard, it—or she; I wasn't sure if the guardian was a fragment of Grandma's actual personality or something else entirely—must be watching closely. And surely a fictional character wandering around town was a security risk, to say the least.

We reached the bottom of the stairs and found Cass peering out of the door to the Magical Creatures Division.

"Oh, good." She eyed the newcomer, who was currently examining one of the enclosed glass cases in which we kept the books that tended to bite people who tried to read them. "He's alive after all."

"He's also fictional," I whispered to her on the way past. "She's officially lost it."

"Lost what?" she asked. "Her sanity? Did she ever have it in the first place?"

"What are you two whispering about?" Aunt Candace beckoned to the vampire, who lifted his gaze from the cabinet. "Jaxon, meet my other niece, Cass. Don't mind the farmyard smell. She keeps magical animals."

Cass narrowed her eyes. "Yes, and they bite."

Jaxon glared straight back at her. Oh boy. While she generally had the sense to avoid picking a fight with the actual local vampires, that might not extend to fictional ones. With an unpleasant jolt, I wondered how many abilities he shared with the vampires I was familiar with. Mind reading, for instance. Cass was protected due to an amulet she'd got her hands on for the purpose of making living under the same roof as one of the living dead more tolerable, but the rest of us were open books. Pun intended.

"Come on, Jaxon," Aunt Candace cooed. "We have lots to see."

The vampire swivelled to her. "Did you say *magical* animals? What are you, traders?"

"No, librarians."

Cass gave a snort, but Aunt Candace pointedly took Jaxon's arm and steered him across the third floor.

I took Cass aside and whispered, "He's a vampire, you know. Might want to avoid picking a fight."

"Of course he is. I recognised him right away."

Ah. She'd read considerably more of Aunt Candace's books than I had, but Cass was usually the first person to raise an objection whenever anything happened that threatened the library's security, and this situation definitely qualified as such. "Doesn't that bother you?"

"Obviously," she said, "but there's no stopping her when

she's in this sort of mood. I'm sure she'll get bored of him eventually and send him back where he came from."

I was less convinced. "A dead body was one thing, but a living vampire? That could make trouble for us in a hundred ways."

She raised a brow. "Living?"

"You know what I mean." I cast a glance at Aunt Candace, who was enthusiastically showing Jaxon the contents of the shelves.

Some of the books snarled and bared sharp teeth at the newcomer, and he hissed right back. When one particularly adventurous book fell off the shelf and began crab crawling towards them, I grabbed my Biblio-Witch Inventory from my pocket and ran my finger down the page to the word *stop*. As the book halted its crawl, Estelle used one of the pincer-like devices propped up near the shelf to return it to its rightful place.

The man stared at us both. "How did you do that?"

"Erm…" I looked to Aunt Candace, wishing I'd read the book she'd summoned him out of so that I knew what kind of magic was safe to use in front of him. Not biblio-witch magic, I was betting. As far as I knew, she'd never put my family's talents into a book.

"It's a gift," she announced to him. "We're very skilled."

Cass snorted again. I gave her a warning look, but Jaxon didn't seem to have noticed her reaction. His gaze panned over the shelves to the balcony and the stairs beyond.

"Seriously," I whispered to Cass, "can you imagine what Evangeline will say when she finds out we have a strange vampire in the library?"

"We already *have* a strange vampire in the library."

"Laney isn't—oh, you meant him." She referred to the vampire who'd been asleep in the basement since our grand-mother's time and whose identity was a mystery even to my aunts. Whatever kind of enchanted sleep he was in, nobody had been able to wake him, and as far as I knew, Evangeline wasn't even aware of his presence here. "Still. What if—"

"Stop with the what-ifs," Cass reprimanded me. "Let her have her fun. It's Christmas."

"Not for another month. And I thought you didn't care." Cass was about as enthusiastic about the holiday season as Aunt Candace was about doing her tax return.

In answer, Cass retreated behind the door to the Magical Creatures Division and firmly closed it behind her. *Great.*

I ran to catch up with Estelle, who wore an expression of mild horror far more appropriate to the situation than her younger sister's indifference "My mum's going to kill her."

"If the guardian doesn't get there first." It was lucky there weren't any visitors up on the third floor, but most people had a healthy aversion to handling the library's fanged and clawed inhabitants and usually asked one of my family members to retrieve any books they needed from up here instead. Given that Cass's magical monsters occasionally got loose, too, that approach was better for everyone.

A fictional character, though, was a new one. And while retaliation from the guardian would come swiftly to anyone who betrayed our secrets, fictional or not, there was also the possibility that Evangeline would take another vampire's presence on her turf as a threat.

Aunt Candace didn't seem to care in the least, while Jaxon himself stared around the library as though he'd landed on an alien planet. Which was a fair reaction. The library had overwhelmed me when I'd first entered too. While I'd come from the normal world and had never encountered anything magical at all before that day, this guy technically came from a world that did have magic, though one that operated on very different rules than this one. And probably did not contain the library.

"Do you have a copy of the book he came from handy?" I whispered to Estelle. "I think we're going to need to become experts on that kind of vampire ASAP."

"I think I have a copy of the first one in my room. I read it years ago."

As Aunt Candace steered Jaxon downstairs, I moved to follow, hoping we didn't have to stop him from wandering into the Dimensional Studies Section on the way to the second floor. He kept stopping to stare over the balcony, though the giant tree blocked most of the view of the ground floor. Atop its peak sat Sylvester, whose presence reminded me I'd completely forgotten that I'd intended to fetch the Book of Questions and conjure him up a tree of his own.

That would definitely have to wait until later. When we reached the second floor, the path downstairs was blocked by my aunt Adelaide. Estelle's mother resembled an older copy of her eldest daughter, sharing the family's curly red hair and dressed in the same silver-lined black cloak. She eyed Jaxon with one eyebrow raised. "And who are you?"

"Now, don't be rude," said Aunt Candace, sidestepping her sister. "This is Jaxon. He's here with me."

Estelle took her mother aside to explain while Aunt Candace led Jaxon on a tour of the second floor. Hoping she'd have the sense to keep him away from the Artefacts Division, I joined Estelle in telling my aunt about the latest unwelcome development.

Aunt Adelaide's expression darkened with every word. When we finished, she waylaid her sister on her way past and snagged her arm, whispering, "You have to return him at once."

"Don't be absurd," Aunt Candace muttered back. "It's not possible for me to make another wish today, and he's not doing any harm, is he?"

"He's not real, Candace."

"Don't say that in front of him. You'll hurt his feelings."

Jaxon himself appeared too fascinated by the nearby shelves and their floating ladders and lanterns to notice their altercation, but I kept an eye on him as I approached them.

"What *did* you tell him?" I asked Aunt Candace. "Did you have an explanation as to why he's here and not in his own story? Telling him he has amnesia won't explain why the rules of *magic* are different."

"I told him that he was hit by a memory spell and that we brought him here to the library to protect him and take care of him until his recovery," she said. "It's more or less true. I think the corridor scrambled his memories of where he came from."

"And are you sure it won't scramble *your* memories when you let someone who's living proof of the corridor's existence roam around town unchecked?"

"I intend to keep a close eye on him," she said. "Frankly, he's safer here than in his own world as the cut-throat leader of a pack of vampires."

"And when the real vampires here find out about him?" Estelle asked. "What do you think Evangeline will do?"

"Nothing whatsoever because he's no threat to her authority," she said. "He's from out of town. You needn't worry. He's used to being around paranormals."

"I can guarantee he's not used to the library." The library was an oddity even in the magical world, and while I'd been completely unprepared when I'd entered for the first time myself, at least I hadn't been conjured into existence by someone looking for a date with a fictional character.

Aunt Candace tutted. "It'll be fine. You need to lighten up. It's Christmas."

"It isn't," Estelle said ineffectually, as Aunt Candace vanished amid the shelves once again. "Maybe putting the tree up early was a bad idea."

"Would waiting have stopped her, though?" Aunt Adelaide shook her head after her sister. "If it's true and she can't get rid of him today, one of us might be able to, but I expect we'd need to take him up to the fourth floor for it to work."

"Seriously?" I arched a brow. "Would Aunt Candace let us haul Jaxon upstairs without a fight?"

"No." My aunt scowled. "I suppose a *day* won't do any harm, but I should have been keeping a closer eye on her. I assumed she'd got tired of the idea of conjuring one of her characters after the first few weeks of trying."

"I didn't even know she'd been trying to bring her characters to life for that long," I admitted. "Or why the guardian let her get away with it. Also, you should know that a couple of local witches showed up earlier wanting to find the hidden corridor because they heard there was a wish-granting book in there. It wasn't *quite* accurate, but supposedly they heard a rumour at the pub."

Alarm flashed across her face. "What did they do?"

"Sylvester shut them in the Dimensional Studies Section, so I pretended that was the hidden corridor," I explained. "Needless to say, they weren't keen to stick around and open any of the books."

"Good." She sucked in a breath. "How on earth did that kind of rumour spread outside the library?"

"No clue, but I guess it's hard to keep that kind of thing a secret." Several people had ended up cursed by the guardian when the corridor had first opened, including Aunt Candace herself, and while it now trusted any member of our family by default, we didn't need the whole world knowing we had a magical wish-granting machine here in the library any more than we needed anyone getting their hands on the Book of Questions.

"I suppose," said Aunt Adelaide. "With any luck, she'll get

bored of this dalliance within a day. Maybe she'll change her mind when he turns out not to be who she thought he was."

"Will that happen, though?" I asked. "I mean, she created him. She made him what she wanted him to be."

"And the library's magic brought him to life," said Estelle. "That's not something we need the whole world finding out, is it?"

"No, and too much of that corridor is an unknown even to our family," said Aunt Adelaide. "I'll go and keep an eye on her. Can one of you watch the front desk?"

"Sure," Estelle and I said at the same time.

"We'll both go," I added, figuring I could pay a visit to the Forbidden Room while I was there.

"I guess it's not the first time something from one of Aunt Candace's books has materialised in here," I muttered to Estelle as we made our way downstairs. "Remember the werewolves from space?"

"Don't remind me," she said. "At least they disappeared when the spell was over."

"Yeah, but we had to go through a few iterations first." That incident had been the product of a Manifestation Curse, which had brought various characters and situations straight out of Aunt Candace's novels and had wrought havoc across the town for days. The other effects had included a love spell that had caused Aunt Adelaide to almost remarry her ex-husband and turn the library into an impromptu wedding venue. Really, dealing with a lone vampire was nothing by comparison.

"I guess," she said. "My mum and Cass are probably right. She'll get bored eventually. She usually does."

"I know, but why a vampire?" I sighed. "We were doing so well at keeping Evangeline's attention off that corridor."

Rumours spreading around the local pub were one thing, but keeping a secret from a group of mind readers with entirely too much curiosity was another matter altogether. Especially when my best friend spent most evenings under Evangeline's watchful eye. While Laney had been practising hiding her thoughts extensively, I figured it was only a matter of time before the vampires' leader figured out the almost literal treasure trove the library sat on. The rare books were enough of a curiosity to her already.

"She might try to recruit him." She shuddered. "I know he's not the same sort of vampire as she is, but still. This isn't good."

"I'm not clear on the distinction, to tell you the truth. I haven't read any of those books." Now seemed an excellent time to catch up, though, and when we reached the lobby, Estelle used her trusty *find* spell to conjure up two copies of the first book in the series.

"The Vampires of Moonfang Cliff," she said, flipping open the first book. "It's been a while, but I remember those vampires don't require an invitation to enter a building."

"That's probably not going to be an issue." For better or worse, as a public building, the library was already accessible to anyone who wasn't barred by my family's extensive security spells. "And the mind reading?"

"No mind reading."

"Oh, good." I flicked through the book. "He has the super speed, though…"

"And can cross running water."

"Not much of that around anyway." Except the ocean, but that apparently didn't count. "Anything else we should keep an eye on?"

"I remember something about…" Her brow furrowed. "Not mind control, exactly, but subtle influence. Like a kind of spell that makes people want to listen to the vampires' leader."

"Seriously?" I spun around, as if we might find the

vampire directly behind us, waiting to put us under his spell. "Okay, that's reason enough to send him packing."

"He also can't go outside during the day at all without bursting into flames," Estelle said. "That means he'll have to stay in the library."

"Only until the sun goes down." And in winter, that would happen earlier rather than later. "Does that mean he should be asleep, as it's daytime?"

"Probably, but he's disorientated enough that he won't know what time it is." She tutted. "Oh, good. It's not that series where the vampires can turn into bats. That must be a different one."

"Yeah, we don't want that."

We continued to thumb through the book and make notes while Aunt Candace took Jaxon on a tour of the upper floors. When she eventually came down to the lobby, the pair of them were chatting amiably. An irate Aunt Adelaide followed them, her mouth pressed in a thin line of disapproval.

"We made a list of what he's capable of," Estelle told her mother after the pair of them had vanished into the living quarters. "He can't read minds, and he also can't leave the library during the day."

"It's what he'll get up to after dark that concerns me."

"Me too." I glanced up at the clock. "Dammit. I already had plans tonight."

"A date with Xavier, right?" asked Estelle. "You should go. We'll keep an eye on Aunt Candace."

"Are you sure?"

"Of course," Aunt Adelaide said. "I doubt my sister will want to stay in the library, and you don't deserve to give up your date because of her."

She was right. Just before I was due to leave on my date with Xavier, Aunt Candace came sauntering into the lobby wearing a new flowery dress. Jaxon accompanied her, dressed in a smart suit. I decided not to ask where she'd got that from.

"I'm going out," she announced. "We're going on a date together."

"It's not a date," I muttered so that only she could hear me. "It's manipulation. You *created* him."

She tutted. "I can't go back and uncreate him now, can I?"

"Yes, you can," said her sister. "Tomorrow."

"Then we might as well enjoy tonight, mightn't we?"

I shook my head. "Where are you going anyway?"

"Out," she said. "I'll let him choose. It'll be somewhere high-class."

At least that meant she wouldn't show up at the Black Dog pub, which was my and Xavier's favoured date spot. While the timing wasn't ideal, the others insisted that it wasn't worth me skipping out on a date with Xavier because of my aunt's antics, and Jaxon himself seemed genuinely happy about getting to see the rest of town. As they left the library, Laney came downstairs. My best friend and newly created vampire slept during the day, so she'd missed the action.

Laney entered the lobby on graceful feet. Her transformation had turned her dark hair glossy and her dancer's figure even more elegant, even while half asleep. Yawning, she gave the Christmas tree an appreciative look. "Nice. Good to see Sylvester's leaving it alone. I know you were worried."

Oops. What with our attempts to scour Aunt Candace's books for details on Jaxon's abilities, I never had got round to summoning the owl a Christmas tree of his own. "Yeah, we reached a compromise. Also, it's not him who's currently causing trouble. Thanks to Aunt Candace, we have a new vampire in town."

Her eyes rounded when I gave her the details of my aunt's

latest scheme. "It's a good job I don't have a lesson with Evangeline tonight," she remarked.

"Tell me about it." If Evangeline had read her mind and deduced Jaxon's presence, I could only imagine what her reaction might be. Laney was practised at shielding her thoughts from the head vampire, but that didn't mean the notoriously perceptive head vampire wouldn't guess something was amiss regardless. "I thought we could do without another vampire-related complication, but evidently Aunt Candace disagreed."

Laney shrugged an elegant shoulder. "He sounds less tricky than the vampires we usually deal with. We don't need to worry about…"

"About him being in league with the Founders? I guess not." A fictional vampire couldn't possibly belong to the group who'd inducted me into the magical world with one of the most terrifying experiences of my life, nor the ones who continued to threaten my family and friends. "We don't need any of *them* getting wind of this either, though."

"Definitely not," she said. "I'll stay local tonight. No roaming."

"Evangeline still has you scouting for trouble?"

"About once a week."

A shiver of unease stirred inside me. Laney was a thousand times more indestructible as a vampire than she'd been as a magic-free human, but Evangeline's infuriating habit of sending her to scout around for the Founders' hiding spots was a constant source of worry. For me, at least. Laney herself was unconcerned about the potential danger and enjoyed stretching the limits of her vampire powers, though she gave me updates after each excursion to reassure me that she'd seen no traces of the Founders since our most recent encounter. That incident was too fresh in my mind for me to forget, although Carlos Verdant and Victoire remained held captive in Evangeline's dungeon while she interrogated them for information on their allies.

"Relax," she said, not needing to read my thoughts to pick up on my anxiety. "It's fine. She mostly uses those missions as an excuse to test me on my vampire powers. Anyway, she won't care about that guy. He's no threat."

"I guess not," I acknowledged. "I know it could be worse too. You weren't here that time half her books came to life, and we had knights and werewolves running amok all over the library. Not to mention the tentacled space monsters."

"Fun," she said. "Do you know which book he came from?"

"This one." I reached for the copy I'd left on the desk. "Estelle and I have been making a list of the differences between him and our own local vampires. There are a lot of them. He can't read minds, for one. He isn't a threat to Evangeline, but that doesn't mean I want her to know he's here."

She might try to win him over, or worse, designate him as a rogue. Neither would end well for Jaxon, nor for Aunt Candace, come to that.

"I won't let her read my thoughts," she said. "If that's a worry."

"Honestly, it's almost easier if she *does* catch Jaxon and put an end to Aunt Candace's fantasies," I admitted. "But life's never that simple."

A knock on the front door indicated my own date's arrival. I said goodbye to the others and greeted Xavier on the doorstep with a kiss. As per usual, he looked as far from an angel of death as possible, with light blond hair and aquamarine eyes, though his black attire and the scythe strapped to his back kind of gave the game away.

"Hey." He smiled. "I just saw your aunt with some guy. Going on a date, is she?"

I groaned. "You don't know the half of it."

Seeing him always cheered me up, and very little fazed the Reaper, so I could give him all the details without him responding with much more than a raised eyebrow.

"Is this even the first time one of her characters has come to life?" he asked when I finished telling him the whole saga.

"No, but last time she was sensible enough to want them gone. Also, she wasn't the instigator."

And they weren't vampires. Which was enough of a potential disaster on its own.

We reached the pub and picked out our usual table. "I worried Aunt Candace would bring Jaxon—the vampire—here," I added as we ordered our food. "But she said she was going somewhere more high-class. Whatever *that* means."

"Good. I like us to have this place to ourselves."

"Me too." We'd been coming here often enough that we didn't attract as many stares as we had at first, for which I was also grateful. After the drama of day at the library, a relaxing, low-key evening was exactly what I needed, and we soon moved to more pleasant topics of discussion, including my latest magic lessons and my discovery of Sylvester's ambition to have his own tree. Xavier found the latter highly amusing.

"At least it'll get him out of your hair," he remarked.

"For the time being," I said. "I got distracted by Aunt Candace's antics and forgot to actually get him the tree, so I need to do that at some point."

We were about to order our second round of drinks when Xavier lifted his head and stared into the distance in the manner peculiar to Reapers. "Oh no. I'm being called to collect a soul."

I suppressed a groan. "Can't your boss go?"

"If he hasn't already, it's up to me." He rose from his seat. "Sorry."

"It's fine." When his Reaper duties called, saying no wasn't an option, and while Xavier and the Grim Reaper had come to a compromise over him dating a human, that didn't include not interrupting our dates with commands to collect the souls of the dead.

I walked with him out of the pub and into the chilly night air. "Whereabouts?"

"The high street. Want me to drop you back at the library?"

"Yes. No, wait." Suspicion stirred. "I'd like to make sure it's nowhere near my aunt and her date." *Please, no.* That was all we needed.

Xavier and I walked across the darkened square, past the towering form of the library and towards the high street branching westward. That was where all the high-class restaurants—or the few that existed in Ivory Beach—were located, but so were a lot of other places. It didn't mean anything, and I gave myself a mental shake to stop my brain from conjuring up worst-case scenarios.

Xavier halted outside a pub called the Cocktail Cauldron. I'd only been in there once, when Xavier and I had been scouting potential alternatives for our dates and had swiftly discovered that it was the meeting place for the local karaoke club. Which meant Aunt Candace *definitely* wasn't in here, at least. She despised the very concept of karaoke.

Xavier sidestepped the pub and ducked down an alleyway, using his stealthy Reaper abilities to creep along towards a beer garden near the back. There, a woman's body lay sprawled on the ground.

Right next to Aunt Candace and her vampire companion.

3

───────

Xavier reached for the scythe he carried strapped to his back. Even having seen him do so countless times, it was still unnerving to watch him go into Reaper mode, moving on soft feet and lifting the scythe over the body of the deceased woman.

As he did so, a ghostly figure floated upward, resembling a transparent mirror of the dead person below. Shadows fanned outward from Xavier's body as the ghost regarded him with a look of confusion. She spoke, but her words were drowned out by a commotion as the other people in the pub crowded outside to see what was going on. Luckily for them, they didn't see the door edged in light that appeared at Xavier's command nor the way the ghostly figure passed through the door into the world beyond. My relationship with Xavier gave me a front row seat to the afterworld, but they probably just saw him, and his scythe, and the body.

"What's going on?" Someone gave a shrill scream. "It's Patti!"

"Is she dead?" asked another.

"The Reaper's here, you dolt," slurred a wizard who was

drunk enough that he could barely keep his feet. "Of course she's dead."

"No!" The first speaker, a female troll with a tangle of swampy green hair, poked the body with a foot. "She's dead. She's dead!"

As shouts rippled amidst the crowd, I edged closer to Aunt Candace. What on earth had possessed her to a pub with karaoke night as a feature when she'd stated more than once that she'd sooner eat her own notebook and pen than listen to someone else's terrible singing? I wouldn't have expected a high-class vampire to care much for this kind of establishment either, come to that, but that was the least of my worries at the moment.

"How did you end up here?" I whispered to her. "What happened to that woman?"

"I haven't the faintest idea."

The fact that this wasn't the first time I'd found a family member next to a dead body should have been kind of worrying, really. "Who is she? Did you know her?"

"I'd never met her before today."

I glanced between her and the vampire. "Wait. Which one of you found the body?'

"Jaxon did."

Oh. Oh no.

"We were having such a good night," she added in wistful tones.

"I thought you hated karaoke."

"Oh, I do," she said. "But Jaxon's singing is divine. I think everyone was jealous of him."

"That's beside the point. Someone's *dead*." I glanced at Jaxon, who stood with the eerie absolute stillness of someone who didn't need to breathe or move. His expression betrayed nothing, and a flicker of suspicion stirred inside me. "How did she die?"

The growing crowd made it hard to see much of the body, but through a gap between two elderly witches, I caught a glimpse of her face. Her head was pillowed on one outstretched hand, blond hair splayed out, mouth slightly open. Wait. I knew her. Wasn't she one of the witches who we'd found in the Dimensional Studies Section earlier? *She was trying to get to the fourth floor.*

I gave myself another mental shake. Jaxon couldn't possibly have known that, could he? Even Aunt Candace didn't.

I moved closer to him. "Ah—you found her like this? You didn't see how she died?"

"No," he replied. "I did not. Have you called the paranormal authorities?"

"You mean the police? I assume someone has." In his own world, there was some kind of independent authority, but I hadn't memorised everything about the system in the world Aunt Candace had created. I certainly hadn't thought I'd need to know anything about how they enforced the law, but I'd got the impression the vampires *were* the authority. Oh boy.

"And you didn't see… anything strange?" I asked, losing my nerve a little at the vampire's unblinking stare. "Or anyone else outside? I mean, she can't have just dropped dead out of nowhere."

"Can't she?" There was a challenging note to his voice that made me wonder if maybe she could have, where he came from. As far as I remembered, in the world of his book series, magic was a skill that anyone could learn by studying from a book and without needing a tool like a wand, and I didn't know if there were any spells that could cause someone to drop dead on the spot.

"Not without a cause," I said firmly. "You didn't see anyone?"

"No, we didn't," Aunt Candace said. "Stop badgering him."

"He found the body," I said out of the corner of my mouth. "I'm not going to be the only person to ask questions."

While I assumed Aunt Candace had come up with a cover story to explain where he'd come from, a grilling from the police was bound to expose that he was no ordinary vampire. And if word got out that he'd walked straight out of a book, a possible murder accusation was the least of our problems.

I glanced at Xavier, who gave me a sympathetic look in exchange. A Reaper was supposed to remain impartial, and I assumed he would have said if Patti's ghost had mentioned the identity of her killer. I made my way to his side anyway and whispered, "Please tell me she saw who killed her. If someone did."

"She didn't," he murmured back. "That man—Jaxon—he found her?"

"Yes, and she was at the library earlier—"

"Police!" someone shouted, and the crowd parted to let Edwin and his troll guards through. The smaller elf was flanked by two huge men with grey skin crammed into suits.

Upon seeing them, Jaxon let out a hiss, displaying sharp fangs. *They come out when the vampire feels threatened.* I recalled this from what I'd read earlier, except the trolls would take his reaction as threatening in turn. When they zeroed in on him, I gave Aunt Candace a look urging her to step in. To my horror, she watched the display with fascination, as though wondering what Jaxon would do next, and in the sudden silence that followed, I heard the distinct scratching noise of her notebook and pen somewhere nearby, her enchanted pen no doubt writing an account on this whole situation so she could transplant it into a book.

It was up to me, then. Approaching Jaxon, I whispered, "They're the paranormal authorities. It's best to answer their questions as honestly as possible if you don't want to get into trouble."

"*They're* the paranormal authorities?" he asked in derisive tones. Oh boy. Given what I'd read of the book series, trolls and elves didn't exist in his world, and he evidently didn't think much of them at all.

"Yes." I glared at Aunt Candace when she snickered behind her hand. "And they're here to find out who killed… Patti, was it?"

"Aurora." Edwin spoke in the usual tone of exasperation he reserved for me and certain of my family members. "I should have guessed you'd be here."

"She was with me," Xavier put in. "I collected Patti's soul."

"And your aunt came along for the ride?"

"No, she was already here." I jerked my head at Aunt Candace. "She can explain."

I hope. Aunt Candace wasn't acting like the pinnacle of innocence either, but I knew *she* hadn't killed Patti. Jaxon, though? If he'd been alone, without any witnesses, when he'd found the body…

"Jaxon found this witch lying dead in the beer garden," Aunt Candace told him. "Looks like she dropped dead. Poison, I'm guessing. I knew those cocktails looked toxic."

"Didn't you drink three of them?" someone asked.

I groaned inwardly, but most of the crowd were too busy exchanging shocked whispers to make note of my aunt's comment. There'd been a surprising number of people crammed into the relatively small room, all dressed up and some carrying bright cocktails in vibrant shades.

"You found the body?" Edwin addressed Jaxon. "And who are you? You aren't local."

"He's new in town," Aunt Candace interjected. "He's visiting. We were on a date."

Edwin eyed him suspiciously. "Were you now? I'll need to

ask you some more questions, but first, can someone tell me what happened here?"

A dozen voices spoke up, offering variations on the same story. Patti had been at karaoke, they'd said, and must have gone outside to get some air. Nobody had any idea when or why; evidently, the singing had been too loud to hear a word anyone said. What *was* clear was that nobody had seen Jaxon before that night, and they didn't know Aunt Candace either.

Edwin's trolls herded everyone back into the pub to better ask questions, and as I'd feared, Jaxon was the first person to be questioned.

"No, I'll go instead," Aunt Candace insisted. "He didn't do anything. He's not from here."

"I just need his account of how he found the body," said Edwin with exaggerated patience. "I would prefer not to have to take either of you into custody."

I glanced at Jaxon, concerned that his fangs would make an appearance again. From his scowl, he didn't assign Edwin any authority in the slightest and didn't appear afraid of the troll guards either, but he did as he was asked and accompanied them to a table in the corner, pursued by Aunt Candace's complaints.

I moved to Xavier's side. "Did her ghost say anything that hinted at how she died?"

"No," he whispered back, "but I can have a look at the body."

"All right." Heart racing, I watched him cross the pub floor on swift Reaper feet while I waited near the bar. Most of the floor space had been cleared to make room for karaoke, and a large stage fitted with a microphone dominated the right-hand side of the pub. The air smelled of fruit cocktails and sweat, and the inebriated state of the crowd did not inspire confidence that anyone would have a clear explanation for Edwin.

Why on earth did Aunt Candace come here? That wasn't the prevailing question, but I had a hard time believing this had been her idea. This place was as far from high-class as you could get, the floors sticky with spilled drinks and a tattooed youth with rainbow-streaked hair occupying the spot of the sole bartender. The karaoke attendees were an odd group, too, including elves and shifters as well as witches and wizards. No vampires—with one obvious exception—and I hoped he'd kept his fangs well hidden.

Xavier returned as swiftly as he'd left. "Her neck was broken. That's what killed her."

"Not poison?" *Broken neck?* "Did she trip? Or…"

"Or was pushed," he said. "I couldn't tell from the angle, but she didn't see her attacker, I don't think. She seemed surprised when I spoke to her ghost."

Who could push someone with that much force? *A vampire certainly could.* "Were there bite marks?"

"No." He spoke in a murmur. "I wondered, so I checked."

"Good." Or not. The lack of bite marks wasn't definitive proof, after all. I looked for Aunt Candace and saw she'd finally stopped trying to get past them to speak to Edwin, so I waylaid her. "Getting in the police's way won't help, you know."

"Jaxon doesn't understand how the legal system in this world works," she protested. "Someone has to help him out."

"Were you there when he found the body?" I dropped my voice. "Did he speak to the witch who died at all?"

Her eyes narrowed. "Now, I know what you're doing."

"You have to admit how suspicious this looks."

Jaxon's character in the book was a tad volatile, to say the least. He'd killed a ton of people on the page, and while that fit with the cut-throat world of the story, acting in that manner in reality would have all-too-real consequences.

She took in a breath. "I'm going to ignore the insinuation,

Rory, if you don't mind. Tonight has been traumatising enough for him already."

"Seriously," I hissed. "What if he gets arrested? You'll have to explain where he came from."

"I most certainly will not."

I had no doubt she could come up with a convincing cover story, but would Jaxon back up her word? The problem with Aunt Candace was that she was stubborn enough that even if she had originally intended to send Jaxon back to his book by the next day, his arrest would likely mean she'd decide to keep him here for another week to teach everyone a lesson.

"Then the consequences will be on you if the guardian decides to wipe your memories again," I said.

"The guardian and I are friends and don't talk about that in public."

"You brought living proof of its existence to *karaoke*. Which you hate. Were you replaced by an impostor when you were up in that corridor?"

"Don't you be smart with me, Aurora," she said. "There's absolutely no reason to connect either of us to this unfortunate death. Neither of us is part of their ridiculous karaoke club."

"Then why exactly are you here?"

"I will suffer through any torture in order to listen to Jaxon's divine singing."

I gave an eye roll. "Don't forget his world operates by different rules than ours."

"I know. I *invented* it."

That's kind of the problem. I hadn't immersed myself in that world long enough to call myself an expert, and while Aunt Candace might have prepared a cover story or three, the truth was bound to come out eventually, one way or another.

I cast my gaze around the gathering patrons, wondering

if any of them would offer any clues pointing to guilt that would get Jaxon off the hook. Almost all of them were drunk enough not to qualify as reliable witnesses, except perhaps the female troll who was now sobbing over the bar. Trolls had to drink a lot more than humans for the alcohol to have any effect.

When Edwin finally let Jaxon go, the vampire made straight for the front door. Aunt Candace hurried over and whispered in his ear.

I crossed the room to join them. "What are you doing? You can't leave."

"Haven't we given enough evidence?" enquired Jaxon. "We should be allowed to walk free."

"That might be how it works in your world, but not here." I looked to my aunt. "Aunt Candace, you know why Edwin will be even more suspicious if you go back to the library without waiting for his permission."

"I didn't ask for a lecture." She glared at me. "And Jaxon didn't either. There's no proof against either of us."

"That doesn't mean you can just leave." I addressed Jaxon. "What did you tell the police anyway?"

Jaxon eyed me. "And what business is it of yours?"

Aunt Candace gave a laugh. "He has a point."

I ignored my aunt and continued speaking to the vampire. "I know my aunt probably didn't tell you this, but in this world, you can get into a lot of trouble for withholding information from the police. I'm trying to help."

Aunt Candace's smirk slid off her face. "Maybe we don't want you to."

"Have some sense," I said. "This isn't a game. Someone's dead, which contrary to what my aunt might have told you, isn't as common here as it is where you came from."

Jaxon eyed me. "I told the police the same as I told you. Isn't that what I should have done?"

"Did you talk to Patti before she died?" I asked. "At all?"

"She spoke to me, yes," he said. "She seemed quite taken with me."

My heart sank. "Did you tell the police that?"

"It didn't seem relevant."

"It kinda was, if you spoke to each other before she died," I said. "Did she ask any questions, or…"

"Stop probing him, Rory," Aunt Candace said. "He already dealt with one interrogation."

"And didn't tell the police the full truth." While I might have put that down to simple ignorance of how things worked here, I had to wonder if Patti had guessed there was something odd about him. She'd already been curious enough to come looking for the corridor at the library, after all, and hadn't she said she initially heard the rumour at the pub?

Had she meant *this* pub? Had someone here been responsible for the rumour that had led her and her friend to the library, and had those same rumours somehow led to her guessing what Jaxon was and that he'd come from inside a book? A vampire would certainly have the raw strength necessary to break someone's neck with their bare hands, given the right incentive, but that line of thinking was a slippery slope.

"I think that's enough from you, Rory." Aunt Candace led Jaxon to a nearby table. "We'll wait here. Go and bother your Reaper boyfriend instead."

Jaxon lifted his head. "Reaper?"

"Yes." Inspiration struck. "He can talk to the dead. Including the one whose body you found. So you know, it's not worth trying to hide anything about what happened to Patti."

He looked stonily back. "There's nothing to tell. I was not responsible for her fate."

Xavier stepped up behind me. "I don't think it's a good idea for me to get my boss involved in this."

"Precisely my thinking." I turned to him and lowered my voice. "I can't believe she isn't taking this seriously."

"Looks like she's been drinking," he murmured back. "She'll come to her senses."

"I hope she does." The rest of the patrons certainly wouldn't. Most were too inebriated to get out much more than a single sentence when the police questioned them, and Aunt Candace herself had little to add to Jaxon's account.

After he'd finished talking to the others, Edwin approached their table. "I'm going to have to take you into custody to ask you some more questions, Jaxon."

Aunt Candace rose to her feet. "Absolutely not."

"This is not your decision, Candace," he said sternly. "I'll ask you both to cooperate."

Jaxon tensed. "Have I not given you all the information you need?"

"No," said Edwin, "you haven't. I'd like you to come with me."

The vampire's fangs appeared again. "I will not be threatened."

"Nobody is threatening you," I said, alarmed. "They just want to talk to you."

The trolls did not look as if they planned to do any talking. Their fists clenched, and they closed in on either side, their own teeth bared.

I grabbed Aunt Candace's elbow. "Is it worth it? Really?"

She shook me off impatiently. "I'll come with him, but this is a waste of time."

Jaxon watched through narrowed eyes. I held my breath, ready to intervene, but he and Aunt Candace followed the police out of the pub without another word.

"That's not good," Xavier murmured from behind me. "We should go."

Yeah. The outright hostile expressions on some of the crowd members as they watched the police depart suggested that Jaxon would be the subject of gossip for the next week, whether he was arrested for murder or not. Though the odds of him committing murder *in* the jail weren't zero either.

Why, Aunt Candace? I asked the same thing at least once every other day, but this was on another level. "She's not being rational at all. I know she's been drinking, and that Jaxon doesn't see murder as a big deal, but she ought to have some level of concern."

"Did he put her under a spell?" Xavier asked. "I can't remember whether you told me if vampires can do that where he came from."

I slammed a hand to my forehead. "Oh, God. I forgot."

I'd completely overlooked that particular advantage, having assumed that my aunt was besotted with the vampire due to her attachment to the fictional love interest she'd created. Not that he'd potentially put a spell on *her.* But hadn't Estelle said he could do exactly that?

"It's not your fault," Xavier said. "You can hardly become an expert on fictional vampires in the space of a day. Anyway, we should leave."

"Agreed." We gladly left the damp pub behind. I half expected to leave a trail of sticky cocktail residue wherever I walked, but the rain soon washed all traces off my shoes. "I can't believe Edwin's about to arrest someone who isn't even real."

"Not necessarily," Xavier said. "I wonder if he'll disappear after a certain amount of time has passed, like that curse last year."

"I wish." Dangerous choice of wording, given where he'd come from. "No, I'm not sure it's the same as that."

If Jaxon disappeared from his cell at midnight, the same way that the subjects of the Manifestation Curse had the previous year, that didn't mean the police would drop their suspicions of my family. And if Jaxon turned out to be the guilty party after all, nobody would ever be able to prove it. Patti's friends and family might never know who'd been responsible for her death.

Though it raised the question of whether a person who wasn't real could legally be arrested for murder at all. The real and unreal blurred on a regular basis in the library, and it was up to the magical law enforcement to figure out who was supposed to take the blame for that. Which, given that the *library* had created him, did not look good for the rest of my family in the slightest.

"On second thought, that would be terrible," I said to Xavier. "If he vanishes, Aunt Candace will probably be arrested in his place."

"Only if he's actually the killer." He gave me a concerned look. "You think he is?"

"He does have a motive—unless someone else does." I shook my head. "The witch who died… she claimed to have heard a rumour at the pub—maybe *this* pub—that we had a hidden corridor in the library that could make people's wishes come true."

His eyes widened. "Oh."

"Exactly."

Might Jaxon—or some other force connected with the library—have gone as far as to commit murder in order to ensure nobody found out the truth? That was a question I couldn't answer.

4

As Xavier and I approached the library, I spied Aunt Candace pursuing the police in the opposite direction, her loud objections echoing across the deserted square.

"I wouldn't follow them," Xavier said, following my gaze. "The way things are going, they'll be at the station all night."

"I know." Yet I also felt a sense of responsibility of sorts, given that Jaxon Hyde was the library's creation. Edwin had no idea, and if Aunt Candace planned to enlighten him at all, there were no guarantees she'd be any more cooperative with his questioning than the vampire would. "The others aren't going to be happy with her."

To say the least. We reached the wide stone staircase leading to the library's entrance, and Xavier kissed me goodnight before I entered the lobby. The library's lower floor was lit with the soft light of the floating lanterns between the shelves, and though we hadn't draped the tree in fairy lights yet, it would look impressive when everything was in place. *Assuming we aren't all behind bars by then.*

Nobody was around, including Laney. If she'd gone out, I

hoped that she was careful. The last thing we needed was the other vampires to get wind of any of this. I didn't know if it was worse if Evangeline heard there was a potential rival in town or that he'd been arrested as a murder suspect.

"You don't look happy." Cass walked out of the living quarters. "Trouble in paradise?"

"Aunt Candace's new boyfriend just got arrested for murder."

"He did what?" Her brows shot up. "He killed someone?"

"Someone died, and he found the body." When Estelle stuck her head out of the living quarters, too, I added, "Is your mum here? She needs to hear this."

"I need to hear what?" Aunt Adelaide's voice drifted out of the living room. "What's your aunt done now?"

"Her boyfriend's been arrested. For murder."

We gathered in the living room, a cosy space between the adjacent kitchen and a staircase leading up to the various bedrooms that either belonged to us or were guest rooms reserved for visitors. And Aunt Candace's research cave, of course. The others listened in tense silence as I explained the events of the night the best I could, including the standoff between Jaxon and the police.

"You don't think he actually did it?" asked Estelle in a hushed voice. "Did Xavier talk to the witch's ghost?"

"She didn't see who killed her," I explained. "Her neck was broken, and I guess whoever was responsible sneaked up on her from behind."

"Vampires have super strength," Cass said.

"I know, but that's not why he was accused," I said. "Aside from the fact that he found the body, he felt threatened and showed his fangs to Edwin's trolls. He also has zero idea how law enforcement works here, and Aunt Candace seems to care more about sparing his feelings than about actually helping the police."

"Does that really surprise you?" Cass enquired.

"No." Aunt Adelaide swore under her breath. "Is she with him?"

"Yeah, she went to the police station."

"Great," said Cass. "More trouble for us."

"Would it have been any better if she'd left him to get arrested without intervening?" I asked.

"He came out of the library," Estelle added. "We're all responsible."

"I never should have let them leave," Aunt Adelaide said. "This is on me. I'll talk to Edwin myself if necessary. Who was the witch who died? Do you know?"

"That's the problem." I took in a breath. "She was one of the two witches I found in the library earlier. The ones who heard a rumour about that corridor and who Sylvester shut in the Dimensional Studies Section."

Estelle sucked in a breath. "She knew—how?"

"She didn't know what the corridor actually was—or where it was either," I added. "Only that it had some hidden ability to grant wishes. But she distinctly said she heard the rumour at the pub. What're the odds that was the same place where she died?"

A tense silence followed, broken by a dismissive snort from Cass. "If you ask me, it sounds like she brought about her own end."

"Cass!" said Aunt Adelaide. "We certainly need to find the source of that rumour, but regardless of where it started, someone is dead."

"Jaxon might not be the murderer, but everyone in the pub was too drunk to talk straight," I explained. "And even if he *was* responsible, who even started the rumour? Aunt Candace had never set foot in there before."

"Obviously, because she hates karaoke," said Cass.

"She claimed Jaxon's singing made it worth putting up

with the rest, but I don't know." I turned to Estelle. "You know the books said vampires could exert some kind of influence over people? That they'd want to listen? Do you think Jaxon might be doing that to her?"

"Oh, it's *those* vampires," Cass said. "Subtle persuasion, isn't it? He can probably use it to get round the police too."

"Well, Aunt Candace isn't being subtle in the least, and neither is he, for that matter. I'd be surprised if one of the trolls doesn't have to knock him out cold to get him into a cell."

"He deserves it," said Cass. "So does Aunt Candace."

"Not if he's mind controlling her, and Edwin doesn't deserve to deal with that either," I said. "He has no idea that the man he's taken into custody isn't even real. I don't know if she plans to tell him, but I mean, can he even legally arrest a fictional character?"

"Sounds like a question you ought to ask Sylvester."

"Don't even." The owl would have a field day with this one. And to top it off, I'd utterly forgotten to ask the Book of Questions to conjure up a Christmas tree. At this rate I'd need to ask for a way to put the whole town under a memory spell that made them forget Jaxon's existence instead.

"This is my fault," Aunt Adelaide said. "I thought my sister would get bored and get rid of him of her own volition."

"I think we all did," Estelle said. "But even if we get rid of him now, someone is dead."

"And who do you think will take the blame?" Cass asked. "If it turns out he did it and the laws say they *can't* arrest someone who isn't real, the person who actually conjured him up will end up jailed in his place. And that goes double if she decides to banish him back to that corridor after all."

Estelle grimaced. "Is there a chance someone else might be the killer?"

"I don't know what to think," I admitted. "Nobody at the

karaoke club confessed, but why would they? They all personally knew Patti. Jaxon didn't."

"I don't care who did it," said Cass. "I care about the library not taking the blame for this."

"I'll go and talk to Edwin," Aunt Adelaide decided. "If we have to explain the truth, so be it."

I agreed. Unfortunately. If Aunt Candace had to pay the price for what her fictional character had done, the library would suffer at least some consequences by default, but what else was to be done? Jaxon himself might not even last out the night, if he ended up vanishing at midnight like the result of the last Manifestation Curse we'd encountered.

I doubted we'd be that lucky, but at least we'd be rid of the possibility of word spreading outside of Ivory Beach that we had summoned up a fictional vampire. Usually, Evangeline was the first to intervene when one of her people got into legal trouble, but he *wasn't* one of her people. And if she claimed otherwise, her own dungeon was the current prison of two dangerous Founders who I most definitely did *not* want to learn of Jaxon's presence in town, nor where he'd come from.

If we didn't solve this one, the consequences would spread far beyond the library.

———

I slept badly that night, not at all helped by Sylvester flying around hooting at random intervals. I'd impulsively decided to ask the Forbidden Room for answers as to whether a fictional person could be arrested, and the owl had simply told me to ask the police. No doubt he'd been insulted that I'd used my daily question for my own purposes instead of keeping my word and getting him his own Christmas tree, but you'd think the current situation would take precedence.

Yawning, I dressed in my usual uniform of casual jeans and a shirt under my silver-lined cloak. The informal attire was a welcome improvement on the old-fashioned getup I'd been forced to wear at my previous job as a bookshop assistant, a memory that stirred more frequently as I approached the one-year anniversary of the day my life had been upended in the best way possible.

I'd known from the very beginning that I would do anything to protect my new life, my new family, and the library.

When I came downstairs, I found a very tired-looking Estelle making breakfast in the kitchen.

"Hey," I said. "I didn't hear your mum come back last night."

"I did." She yawned. "I left my door slightly ajar so I could hear."

"With Sylvester swooping around making a racket?"

"Was he?"

"You must have slept really heavily to miss that," I remarked. "Who even cares about his Christmas tree when the library's secrecy is at risk?"

Sylvester flew overhead, clipping my shoulder with a taloned foot before landing straight on top of the toaster. "Well, *that's* not nice. I'm not to blame for your aunt's ill-advised decision to summon up one of her fictional creations, am I?"

"Sylvester, your feathers will catch on fire," Estelle protested, swatting him away from the toaster. "And nobody was blaming you."

"Also, if you wanted to, you could have easily stopped Aunt Candace and Jaxon from leaving the library," I added. "More than the rest of us. Just saying."

Sylvester extended his wings, causing a stack of plates to wobble. Estelle hastened to rescue them while he spoke in a booming, authoritative voice. "I am the embodiment of the library's entire store of knowledge. You should speak to me with more respect."

"What on earth is going on in here?" Aunt Adelaide entered wearing a dressing gown and with her curly hair piled on her head. "Sylvester, get off the toaster. You'll catch on fire."

The owl puffed out his chest. "I am the—"

"The embodiment of all knowledge, we get it," I said. "You're also sitting on our breakfast."

The owl gave an exaggerated sigh and took flight, settling on top of a cupboard instead. "You have no sense of fun whatsoever."

"Have you forgotten Aunt Candace? Is she still at the jail?" I asked Aunt Adelaide, who'd moved to help Estelle with breakfast.

"Edwin decided to keep Jaxon overnight," she said around a yawn, "and my sister wouldn't leave either. I think she slept on the floor."

That figured. "He didn't start any fights in the jail, did he?"

"Not that I saw."

"And I assume he didn't vanish at midnight."

"No," she said. "I was there until nearly one a.m."

I guess it was a long shot. I took a stack of plates and began setting the table. "Did the police bring in any other suspects from the pub?"

"No, but they were all in such a drunken state that they were unable to answer his questions," Aunt Adelaide said. "I expect he'll talk to more of them today."

"Jaxon will be asleep during the day, won't he?" asked Estelle. "I reread the books overnight, and it sounds like vampires of his sort typically pass out cold at dawn. Might be tricky to question him in that state."

"That's what I thought," I said. "Also, even if the police decided to let him go, he can't set foot outside in daylight without catching on fire."

"Wouldn't that resolve your problems nicely?" Sylvester asked.

"Not the issue of someone spreading rumours about the library behind our backs," I said. "Rumours that led to someone being killed."

Aunt Adelaide flashed me a concerned look. "We don't necessarily need to conclude the worst. An ordinary explanation for that woman's death is still plausible. There were a lot of people in that room in various states of drunkenness."

"Yes, but only one of them wasn't..." I trailed off, not quite daring to say the word *real*. Sylvester filled the gap with a loud cackle.

"I would pay to see your aunt's reaction if she heard that."

"You're an owl. You don't use cash." Not much of a diversion, but he was right: I didn't dare mention my theory in front of Aunt Candace, especially with her possibly under some kind of vampiric mind control. "Aunt Adelaide, does Edwin have any idea that the man he's arrested came from a book?"

"Your aunt made it clear that she intends to break the news to Edwin herself," Aunt Adelaide said. "If she desires to, that is. Otherwise, he remains in the dark."

"For the time being." If Jaxon came out as guilty, he'd be exposed one way or another, but I had to admit that I had a hard time believing Aunt Candace would be acting so flippantly if she thought Jaxon was actually the killer, even if she *was* under his influence. "I wonder... I mean, if he can subtly influence people to listen to him, would it work on Edwin too?"

"It might." Estelle's expression clouded. "He doesn't use

the ability that often in the book. That's why it slipped my mind."

"I wouldn't assume he's using his abilities on the police," Aunt Adelaide said. "If he had a strong influence on Edwin, he wouldn't have been taken into custody, I imagine."

"True," I acknowledged, figuring that Jaxon would have also had a hard time putting Edwin under any kind of hypnosis while in the comatose sleep of a vampire. "But Aunt Candace must have come up with a hell of a cover story to explain why he has no idea how anything works here. He's never even met an elf before."

"I gather the police thought he was an eccentric visitor from another group of vampires who don't have much contact with the outside world," said Aunt Adelaide.

"A *really* eccentric one," Estelle said. "What are we going to do all day while we wait for Edwin to question him? If he doesn't wake up until sundown, he'll be stuck there for the duration, and so will Aunt Candace."

I'd been thinking the same. "I hope Edwin is preparing to question some of the others who were at karaoke too."

"So do I." Aunt Adelaide finished setting the table and pulled out a chair. We sat down to eat, though nobody had much of an appetite.

Sylvester swooped onto the table and stole a piece of toast. "I do hope you plan to fulfil your promise, Aurora."

"I will." I put down my coffee mug. "I don't suppose you know if a character conjured up by the fourth-floor corridor has a time limit, or will he only disappear when Aunt Candace decides to get rid of him?"

The owl hooted loudly. "I will not be insulted!"

"Ow." I covered my ears. "I was only asking a question."

The fourth floor was usually a sore point with him though. He claimed that its wish-granting abilities encroached on the territory of the Book of Questions. I didn't entirely believe him, and I suspected most of the issue was that he prided himself on knowing everything about the library, and learning the corridor had hidden itself in plain sight had been a knock to his pride.

"What did you promise him?" asked Aunt Adelaide.

"To conjure him a Christmas tree of his own so he stops messing with ours," I explained.

"Oh, I can do that," she offered.

"I think he specifically wants me to do it, which wouldn't be an issue, if not for…" I gestured at the world in general.

"We had more important questions to ask first," Estelle said. "You'd think he'd have stopped being so sensitive about that corridor by now. It's not a threat to him."

"Might be, if one of its inhabitants gets us all exposed." We needed to find the source of that rumour, too, though I didn't even know where to begin looking.

When we finished breakfast, Aunt Adelaide rose to her feet first. "I'm going to speak to Edwin. I think we should tell him the truth."

"No way," I said. "He might be able to keep a secret, but what if Evangeline hears that there's a vampire from out of town in jail? She'll walk in there and read his mind right away."

"I won't mention the corridor," Aunt Adelaide decided. "Just that he was a creation of the library. There's no other way to explain the gaps in his memory and knowledge, and it'll help the investigation run much smoother if Edwin has a full understanding."

I had my doubts. "Only if Jaxon cooperates. And what about whoever is spreading rumours about the fourth-floor corridor?"

"Yes, we'll deal with that too." She turned to her daughter. "If we're late back from the police station, can you open the library?"

"Of course," Estelle said. "I was going to offer to do the same."

"You want me to come with you?" I asked my aunt, surprised. "I know I was at the pub, but I didn't see much."

"I think Edwin might be more willing to listen to two of us," said Aunt Adelaide. "Candace, too, though after a night sleeping on the floor of the holding cells, she might have changed her mind about digging her heels in."

Estelle raised a brow. "Not so sure about that. To her, anything is a research opportunity."

"She was probably taking notes all night," I agreed. "All right, let's go."

Outside, it was another cold, drizzly November day. While a few shops had put up their Christmas decorations early like we had, the general mood was more damp than festive. We crossed the square and ducked down the street alongside the clock tower to the seafront, where the police station sat on the corner. The redbrick building was compact, consisting of a single reception room, a few small interrogation rooms off to the side, and an adjacent jail through the door at the back. Edwin sat alone at the desk, looking as tired as the rest of us felt. His eye twitched when he saw us enter.

"Please tell me you've come to collect Candace," he said.

"She isn't locked up?" I asked.

"No, I am not." Aunt Candace's voice drifted through the jail door a moment before she stepped into the reception area. "I'm here to support Jaxon."

"Is he asleep?"

"Yes, he is," said Edwin. "As I told you, I'm afraid I can't possibly let him out until I've conducted a proper question-ing, which seems to be rather difficult at the moment."

Aunt Candace sniffed. "I've been perfectly angelic, and so has Jaxon."

I suppressed a snort. "Ah, Edwin, is there anyone else you have listed as a suspect from the people who were at karaoke night?"

Edwin exhaled on a sigh. "No, but nobody could definitively confirm that they never left the room during the time Patti was killed."

Hmm. While everyone had been drunk enough that their reports would be muddled at best, they'd at least known the victim better than Jaxon had. "Did you confirm how she died?"

"Broken neck," he said. "It's hard to conclude how it occurred. From her position, she might have slipped or was pushed, but the force required suggests that someone with an uncommon level of strength was responsible."

So... not a human. My mind flickered back to the pub. Most people present had been human but not all of them. Even a werewolf could break someone's arm with ease, and hadn't there been a troll there too?

"Ah, Xavier said the same." I didn't quite dare meet my aunt's eyes. "I don't think Jaxon will wake up until dusk, so it might be worth asking if any of the other people present remember more now that they're sober."

"You expect me to wait until dusk?"

"Yes," said Aunt Candace. "I'm sure you can find someone else to question before then."

He puffed out a breath. "I thought most vampires could at least function during the day, if necessary."

"Not this one," I said. "Sorry. I wish it was otherwise."

He eyed me. "Does Evangeline know he's visiting town?"

"No," said Aunt Candace in ominous tones, "and I'm assuming you don't want her to find out."

"If one of her fellow vampires commits a crime, she made it quite clear that she'll be the one to enact punishment."

"He didn't commit a crime, and he's not one of her people," Aunt Candace said. "As a matter of fact, he's mine."

"I don't need to know that."

"That's not what she means." I gave my aunt a significant look. "She—"

"I created him," Aunt Candace finished.

Edwin blinked. "You did what?"

"It was a spell," Aunt Adelaide added. "He's a fictional character from one of her novels."

"He's... what?" He blinked again, jaw slack. "You're joking."

"I'm afraid not," I said. "Sorry."

"I knew he seemed familiar." He looked over his shoulder towards the jail. "Ah, *which* series, exactly?"

"The Vampires of Moonfang Cliff," Aunt Candace supplied. "See, you can't arrest him now, can you?"

His jaw twitched. "What? Being a fictional character doesn't make one immune from the law."

"Is that actually covered under the regular laws?" I asked, curious despite myself.

"No, but a woman is dead." His scowl returned. "You mean to tell me your library summoned up a fictional creation again, after the last time?"

"Last time was an accident." I stopped, figuring that it would not help matters to remind him that Aunt Candace had conjured one of her fictional creations on purpose this time. I really needed some more sleep. "Anyway, there's a chance he might disappear like the last ones did." A slim one, admittedly, but it was there.

"I don't..." He looked helplessly around. "The responsibility, in that case, would lie with the person who was behind his creation."

"My deceased mother," said Aunt Candace. "She created the library."

And you used it. As well she knew, but we were treading dangerously close to exposing the corridor's true capabilities.

"Aunt Candace," I said pointedly, "the only way to stop this is to find out who was responsible, isn't it? And there were a lot of people in that pub."

"Yes, there were," said Edwin. "And I intend to question some of them *if* you and your family members allow me to. If you'd like to take your aunt home with you, Rory, it'll be much appreciated. I will let you know if I need to question any of you again."

Aunt Adelaide silenced her sister's arguments with a pointed stare and steered her out of the police station. When we reached the square, Aunt Candace veered towards the high street instead of the library.

I ran after her. "You aren't going back up to the pub?"

"Someone has to look at the crime scene."

"Yeah, like the police." While being at the pub would be an improvement over her hanging around the station annoying Edwin, he wouldn't be thrilled at her visiting the crime scene either. "Nobody will be there now."

"Precisely," she said. "Anyone who returns to the scene will have a guilty conscience by default."

Aunt Adelaide tutted. "I doubt anyone will be there at this time, but if the staff are around, it might be worth asking for the source of those rumours."

"Oh." Not a bad idea, now she suggested it. "Aunt Candace, if you didn't know, someone was spreading rumours about the library that came pretty close to what the fourth-floor corridor can actually do."

"Rumours?" she echoed. "That's nothing. Someone starts a new rumour about the library every week."

"Except one of the people who mentioned those rumours is the witch who died," I said. "She and her friend were in the library a few hours beforehand. They'd almost made it up to the fourth floor when Sylvester diverted them into the Dimensional Studies Section."

She gave a laugh. "Serves them right."

Had she not made the mental leap between Patti being in the library and later turning up dead? "Well, they claimed to have heard the rumour at the pub."

"Lucky we're going there, then," said Aunt Candace. "It'll be easier to hear ourselves think without that ghastly singing too."

"We?" I echoed.

Aunt Adelaide gave me a searching look. "I wouldn't usually ask this of you, Rory, but I think Candace will require supervision."

"Of course," I said. "I can make sure we don't get under anyone's feet, but there's no guarantee the staff will actually let us in."

"I beg to differ," said Aunt Candace. "The pub is open seven days a week, with karaoke on six nights. This is a minor setback, nothing more."

"Someone died," said Aunt Adelaide. "I wouldn't call that minor in the slightest. However, if you're right, the staff might appreciate the warning that certain… other individuals might take an interest."

Meaning the vampires. "Evangeline. She… well, I know Edwin doesn't want her to know, but she usually takes responsibility for punishing the ones who commit crimes. And the vampires' home is pretty close to the high street."

"Precisely," said Aunt Candace. "I rather expected she might show up at the police station last night, but it seems word has yet to reach her ear."

"That's why you spent the night in jail?" I'd thought she was trying to get under Edwin's feet or had been dazzled by her attachment to Jaxon, but maybe there was some method to her madness after all. "Speaking of rumours, we really do need to find out if someone at that pub was whispering about the library behind our backs. And how much they know."

"I like the way you think." Aunt Candace grinned, her notebook and pen bobbing at her side. "Let's go and investigate."

What have I got myself into?

5

We reached the high street and made our way to the Cocktail Cauldron. The pub shouldn't be open at this hour, but Aunt Candace pushed open the door and strode right in.

As I'd expected, the place was empty, though the same bartender from the previous night was behind the counter, idly polishing a glass. Even during the day, the place smelled strongly of fruit magical cocktails.

The bartender looked up in surprise when we walked in. "Oh, we're technically closed."

"Sorry." I hastened to catch up with my aunt at the bar. "We can come back later."

The bartender ran a hand through his spiky hair. I was pretty sure he was wearing the same faded black T-shirt as the previous night, on which a name tag read Shaw Junior.

"You were there last night," Aunt Candace said to him. "We were hoping to ask some questions."

I groaned inwardly. If he'd been the only fully sober person present last night, he might have more to say than the people who were at karaoke, but not if Aunt Candace insisted on applying an approach with the subtlety of a sledgehammer.

His brow furrowed. "Did the police send you?"

"No."

"Kind of," I amended. "We're from the library, and the witch who was killed was one of our patrons."

Aunt Candace gave me a smirk that made me feel doubly guilty for stretching the truth, even if I had a good reason for it. "That's right."

"Oh." His shoulders hunched. "What d'you want to know?"

"Who was she?" I asked. "Patti, I mean? Did she come here often?"

"Sure, most evenings," he said. "She and her friends were regulars at karaoke."

"Her friends." I leapt on the chance. "Who was the other witch she was with? The one with the pink hair?"

"Corrine, I think," he said. "I don't always remember their names, but neither do they, after a few cocktails." He gave an awkward laugh.

"Do you work here *every* day?" Aunt Candace asked. "I don't see any other staff."

He shifted on his feet as if uncomfortable. "My dad owns the place. Usually, we aren't that busy."

"Except on karaoke nights?" I surmised. That was still six nights a week, which seemed a lot for two people to handle.

"Our last bartender quit," he mumbled. "We're between staff. Ah, I don't know if I can be of much help to you. I didn't know Patti that well."

"You were working alone last night. You didn't see Patti leave the bar?"

"No," he replied. "Didn't know anything was happening until everyone started running outside. It was too crowded to notice much before then."

"And noisy," added Aunt Candace. "You forgot that part."

"Ah, I was wearing an earplug charm," he said with a slightly sheepish expression. "I know everyone's regular orders well enough that I don't need to be able to hear."

"And you don't have to listen to their singing." Aunt Candace gave a cackle. "I assume you didn't see anyone follow Patti outside?"

"No, I didn't even see her leave," he said. "I can't imagine anyone else was paying close attention. Including Patti herself, given how drunk she was."

That was true. Everyone had been loaded except for him and possibly Jaxon. I hadn't checked whether vampires in the book series could actually get drunk, but they usually had a harder time getting intoxicated than humans did.

"Someone was paying attention," Aunt Candace said. "Whoever killed her. Know anyone who might have held a grudge?"

He winced. "I don't know. I'm not an expert."

"You must have some idea, if you've been here every day," said Aunt Candace. "Was Patti a good singer?"

"He was wearing an earplug charm, remember?" I muttered. "Also, it doesn't matter if she was a good singer or not, does it?"

"To the karaoke club, it does," she said. "Maybe someone was jealous of her."

"Might be." His forehead scrunched up. "She wasn't a troublemaker, but once she fell asleep at the bar, and I had to wake her up."

"That doesn't sound like much." I hesitated, on the brink of asking if he'd heard the rumours, but his earplug charm would extend to blocking him from overhearing any conversations too.

"I gather there were a few rivalries among karaoke's

regular attendees," said Aunt Candace. "Did anyone have reason to want her dead?"

"I haven't the faintest idea," he said, looking uncomfortable. "Her death might have been an accident."

"It might have," I acknowledged. "Aunt Candace, I think we should go back to the library."

"I would like to look at the crime scene first," she said.

The bartender made a small noise of protest then shrugged. "Go right ahead."

I gave him an apologetic look and followed my aunt to the door at the back. As I'd expected, there was nothing in the beer garden to suggest how Patti had died.

"She might have tripped," I said dubiously. "But it's more likely she was hit with magic from behind. Or pushed by someone really strong."

"I counted at least three werewolves and a troll among the karaoke's attendees." Aunt Candace's lips pursed. "I'll think on it."

To my relief, she left the beer garden after another cursory glance and made her way across the pub to the front door. The bartender looked equally relieved to see us go.

"Nice job, Rory," she said approvingly. "We'll make a detective out of you yet."

"Didn't know that was the goal." I huddled inside my cloak as a chill breeze swept down the high street. "It's annoying that he was wearing an earplug charm."

"I'd do the same in his place."

"You went there voluntarily," I pointed out. "Also, I meant that he might have been able to tell us the source of the rumours. Unless you heard anything?"

"Rumours?"

"You know, what I said earlier," I said. "Someone told those two witches that there was a book hidden on the fourth floor that can grant wishes. Sound familiar?"

"I thought that owl took care of our overly curious witches."

"Your sister wants to know where she heard the rumour in the first place—and so do I," I added. "If Patti and her friends were regulars at karaoke night, that's got to be the pub they were talking about."

"We'll just have to come back tonight, won't we?"

Oh boy. At least Aunt Candace didn't take any more detours on the way back to the library, and when we entered, she went straight to the living quarters and upstairs.

"Good. You're back." Aunt Adelaide sat behind the front desk, sorting through a pile of returns. "Did you manage to talk to anyone?"

"We talked to the bartender, and he said he had a sound-proofing spell on last night, so he didn't hear anything," I explained. "Everyone was drunk anyway, including Patti. She's the witch who died."

"Did you ask about the rumours?" she asked. "I suppose he wouldn't have heard anything if he was wearing a sound-proofing spell."

"Exactly," I said. "I did find out the name of the witch who was here with Patti in the library. Her name's Corrine, but I don't know if she's a possible suspect or not."

"I hope she's on the police's list of people to question," said Aunt Adelaide. "They'll have plenty of time if Jaxon's asleep all day. Though when he wakes up, I hope he cooperates and doesn't leave out any key information this time around."

That's what I'm afraid of. "He doesn't seem to grasp the concept of a police investigation. And… well, there's still a non-zero chance he *did* do it. Even if he was possibly defending the library's secrecy in the process."

"Exactly," she said in grim tones. "I'll have to keep an eye on my sister to make sure she doesn't try to sneak back to the police station."

"I'll help. Where's Estelle?"

"She was checking on the tree."

"I hope Sylvester didn't get to it again." Oh no. "I'll find her."

I found Estelle at the foot of the Christmas tree, standing in a puddle of tinsel. "Three guesses who's responsible for this?"

"Sylvester." I lifted my gaze and saw him perched on a lower branch.

When he caught me looking, the owl ruffled his feathers. "Remembered I existed, did you?"

"I was busy trying to stop our family from getting arrested," I informed him. "It was urgent. And I apologised for not asking the right question last night. There was no need to ruin all Estelle's hard work."

"We can fix it, no worries," she said. "And I told you, Sylvester, Rory will help you."

"Right now," I added, sensing that the owl would accept nothing less. "Provided you behave yourself in the meantime."

I returned to the front desk. "Is the Book of Questions here?"

Aunt Adelaide looked up from the books she was sorting. "My sister took it."

I groaned. "Typical."

Sylvester swooped in behind me and landed on the shelf overlooking the desk. "Well?"

"You must know Aunt Candace has the Book of Questions," I said. "No doubt she's searching for ways to get Jaxon off the hook."

Which the owl should know, given that he was both

inside the room and outside of it at the same time—a fact that made my head spin if I thought too hard about it.

"You forgot about me. My feelings were hurt."

I surpressed a snort with difficulty. "I'm sure you'll survive."

"*You* might not."

His tone was entirely too ominous for my liking. "I'll get it from her when she's finished."

"I'll hold you to that."

He wasn't kidding. The owl shadowed me as I helped Aunt Adelaide put the returns back into place on the ground floor. It was impossible to get anything else done with him hovering over my shoulder, so when I'd finished returning the students' textbooks to their proper places, I reluctantly made for the living quarters and the stairs up to Aunt Candace's research cave.

My aunt's workspace lay at the very top of the living quarters, behind a door that often bore a sign that said Do Not Disturb or a more alarming version of the same kind of sentiment. Today it said Plotting in Progress. Hoping that meant her novel and not a jailbreak, I knocked on the door.

"What?" asked Aunt Candace's disgruntled voice from the other side.

"Do you have the Book of Questions? I need to borrow it."

She gave a loud sigh. "Can't you use it later?"

"Not if I want Sylvester to leave me alone." As if to prove my point, the owl fluttered down to land on the stairs behind me.

"Fine." She opened the door. "Really, it's hardly as urgent as saving someone from a lifetime of cruel imprisonment."

"That's a bit of an exaggeration, isn't it?" I reached out a hand for the book, a leather-bound tome with nothing on the cover except for a silver question mark. "I won't need it for long anyway."

With Sylvester blocking the way downstairs, I had more of an incentive to open the book there and then on the spot. "I wish to enter the Forbidden Room."

The book's blank pages stared at me for a long moment, and then I toppled headfirst through emptiness. I landed flat on my back, staring at a blank whitewashed ceiling. The whole room usually matched, but today, the walls were draped in tinsel and wreathed in holly. I lifted my head and asked the owl, "Is this what you did with all the decorations you stole?"

No answer followed, though the tinsel rustled as I pushed to my feet. "You already decorated this place. What did you need my help for?"

A skein of tinsel lifted itself off the wall and wrapped around my legs, causing me to stumble and trip over my own feet. "All right, all right. I'll ask my question."

"Go on." The owl's voice echoed from the walls. "I'm waiting."

I took in a breath and did my level best not to trip over onto my face. "My question is, how can I conjure up a tree that will satisfy Sylvester?"

"I would prefer to be referred to by my proper title."

"Proper title?" What game was he playing this time? "What's that?"

"The supreme overlord of the Forbidden Room."

"All right." I tried not to laugh. "How can I conjure up a tree that will satisfy the supreme overlord of the Forbidden Room?"

"You've already asked your question."

"And you didn't answer." I waited. "Come on. You wanted me in here, didn't you?"

"You're boring when you're compliant."

"You'd really rather have an argument?" Honestly. "I asked

my question: how do I conjure up a tree that will satisfy you?"

"Like this."

The room tipped upside down. I tumbled, the tinsel coming free of my legs. I landed on my back outside Aunt Candace's room with my head dangling over the top of the stairs, blinking up into my aunt's face.

"That was fast," she said. "I assume you got what you wanted?"

"I hope so." I rose upright, handing her the book. "Out of curiosity, what did you plan to ask? Not just how to get Jaxon out of jail, I hope."

"What else would I possibly ask?" Her disbelieving tone reminded me that she wasn't entirely acting of her own volition. How far under the vampire's spell was she? More to the point, how long would it last? With Jaxon behind bars, she might come back to her senses at some point, and I hoped it would be sooner rather than later.

Downstairs, someone screamed. Estelle. "Oh no."

Heart sinking, I ran downstairs and into the lobby. A giant tree sat where the reception desk used to be, its roots spanning the research section and its branches extending all the way up to the ceiling.

"Rory!" Estelle peered between branches, her expression alarmed. "The tree—the other one—is going to collapse!"

From the alarming creaking noises behind, she was right. "Sorry. It's my fault. I should have known the only thing that would satisfy Sylvester would be a tree as big as the library itself."

"Really?" She crawled out from underneath the branches and spoke to the newly conjured tree. "Sylvester, don't be silly. We can't let any people into the library with this tree in the way."

"He's in that sort of mood. He actually got angry with me for *not* arguing with him." I rolled my eyes. "I wish I'd asked for help with Aunt Candace and Jaxon instead. That would have been more productive."

"Yes, it would have." Aunt Adelaide crawled out from under the tree and held up her Biblio-Witch Inventory. "Let's see if I can shrink this."

A loud hooting noise came from the tree, and the owl stuck his head out. "Don't you dare."

"We can't let anyone into the library with a giant tree in the way, Sylvester," said Aunt Adelaide. "Be reasonable."

"Also, I thought you wanted to sit on top of the tree," I pointed out. "You can't do that when it's on a level with the ceiling, can you?"

"That won't do," he agreed. "I *suppose* I might be able to compromise, provided my tree is bigger than the other one."

"Well, of course." I gestured to the tree. "Just make it so that people can get to the stairs, at the very least."

"I shall oblige." There was a popping sound, and the tree shrank to a more manageable size. Luckily, no bookshelves had been damaged by the tree's sudden appearance, though several mildly shell-shocked students crawled out from underneath, covered in pine needles. The owl immediately flew upward to land on the top, looking imperiously down at us.

"That's better," Estelle said. "Did Aunt Candace get anything out of the Book of Questions, Rory?"

"I think she was deciding what to ask," I said. "She's so far under the vampire's spell that she can't think about anything else. Will it eventually lose its effects while they're apart?"

"Good question. I can check." She reached for the stack of Aunt Candace's paperbacks she'd left on the desk. "Sorry you ended up having to handle her alone at the pub."

"It wasn't a complete loss. We did speak to the bartender,"

I said. "His dad owns the pub. He didn't give us much in the way of clues about the murder, though, as he was wearing an earplug charm."

"Then he won't have heard the rumours either." She glanced at her mother, her gaze clouded. "I wish I knew how that got out. The corridor erased the memories of anyone who trespassed inside, didn't it?"

"That's what I thought too." The guardian had even enacted the same punishment on Aunt Candace until she'd proven that we were all Grandma's relations and therefore trustworthy. "Ah, have you seen the guardian recently?"

"No, but I haven't been upstairs," she replied. "Cass might have."

"She might," agreed Aunt Adelaide. "Or not. I'm not sure if she's been to the fourth floor recently."

"Aunt Candace said she wished for the room to dispose of a pile of manticore dung."

"She didn't, did she?" Aunt Adelaide shook her head. "I suppose that does at least have a practical use, unlike my sister's antics."

I figured it was worth asking, and since we didn't have many visitors, I decided to go upstairs to check. I was kind of surprised Cass hadn't appeared during the tree's sudden arrival, but I figured she was used to ignoring the noise from the rest of the library while she was with her animals.

When I reached the third floor, I walked to the Magical Creatures Division and knocked on the door. While it was generally unlocked, Cass had a tendency not to give advance warning when she took her manticore out for a walk.

"What?" Cass appeared in the doorway. "You're covered in tinsel."

"Sylvester," I said in explanation. "Just wondered... have you seen the guardian lately?"

"No, but I've hardly left this room. Any reason?"

"I figured it—she?—ought to know if someone is spreading rumours about the library's hidden corridor," I explained. "The murder victim was—"

"One of the two people who Sylvester trapped in the Dimensional Studies Section. I know."

"Who heard a rumour at the pub," I added. "Aunt Candace claimed it was a coincidence that she and Jaxon ended up there, but I don't buy it."

"What? You think he picked that place based on intuition?" she said. "Is it possible?"

"I have no idea, but it's a weird coincidence all the same," I said. "And so is the fact that the person who died is one of the two witches we found in the library."

"If Jaxon was the one who killed her, he's securely behind bars, isn't he?" she said. "He can't do the same to anyone else."

"Yes, but he still *killed* someone," I said. "Also, Aunt Candace told Edwin he isn't real."

She arched a brow. "Did she now?"

"She didn't mention the corridor," I added. "Just that he came out of her book. Which Edwin has read, so he might have worked it out anyway, given enough time."

"And he won't be the last," she said. "It's not her most popular series, but a lot of the locals have read Aunt Candace's books by now. Anyone who asks Jaxon too many questions might work it out."

"Nobody can ask him questions while he's behind bars, but we need to get rid of him."

"Does Aunt Candace agree?"

"No, but he has her under mind control. Or something like it."

"Oh." She swore under her breath. "Right. *That.*"

"Now do you see why I need to find the guardian?" I glanced towards the door to the fourth floor, which was bright green today. "I'll see if she's around."

After opening it, I climbed up the short staircase and scanned the corridor. "Ah, guardian?"

No response came, nor any signs of the ghostly figure that looked like a cross between a book wraith and a Reaper. The guardian kind of creeped me out—I wouldn't lie—but its purpose was to protect the corridor's secrets.

With no answer forthcoming, I dug in my pocket for a pen and walked to the door to the wish-granting room. Wishing for Jaxon to disappear would be unambiguous enough, but something nagged at me all the same. Guilt, maybe, for going behind Aunt Candace's back.

It's for the best. I pressed the pen to the wooden surface.

"I wouldn't," Sylvester said over my shoulder.

I jumped, causing a scribbly line to appear on the door. "I hope that doesn't count as a wish."

"Unless you speak dragonish, you're fine."

"That's not dragonish," I said. "You made that up. Also, since when did you come in here? I thought you hated this place."

"I'm simply indifferent."

"Uh-huh. Have *you* seen the guardian—don't claw me." I backed away when he raised a taloned foot. "She's the one who protects this place and its secrets. I thought she'd be out there at the pub looking for clues."

"I might have expected the same of you," he said. "You're wasting your time by wishing for that mockery of a vampire to disappear, however."

"Why, because he's not here at the library? Does he have to be present to go back into the room?" Did Sylvester have some idea of how it worked after all? He might. The corridor was such a sore point with him that we generally tried to avoid mentioning the subject.

The owl gave no answer. *That's a yes, then.*

"What would you suggest I write, then? And don't say

nothing. I need to solve this problem, and I already had to use up my one question today. Otherwise, if you don't have any advice to offer…"

"I did," he said. "I'm advising you to go downstairs and forget all about this."

"I can do the first part but not the second." I put the pen back into my pocket. "Are you sure that's the best course of action?"

"Need I remind you that I'm the most intelligent being in the library?"

"Of course you are." I hadn't thought through my wish, admittedly, so I went back downstairs and closed the door behind me.

Sylvester swooped over the balcony and settled on top of the newly conjured tree while I descended the stairs all the way down to the lobby and found Estelle levitating a pile of tinsel across the Reading Corner.

"This showed up out of nowhere," she said.

"Probably Sylvester. He was hiding it in the Forbidden Room," I explained. "He's still in a weird mood. He warned me off using the fourth-floor corridor to banish Jaxon."

"You went to the fourth floor?" she asked.

"Briefly," I said. "Sylvester told me not to bother making another wish, so I didn't. I couldn't think of one anyway, and apparently, I can't banish Jaxon when he isn't in the library."

Her brow wrinkled. "I thought Sylvester hated that place."

"So did I. I'm not sure what's going on up there, but I couldn't find the guardian either."

"She's pretty elusive, isn't she?" she said. "Also, it's probably for the best that you didn't banish Jaxon before Edwin could question him properly."

"Assuming he cooperates this time," I said. "I hope Edwin's talked to some of the others too."

"Send Jet to check," she suggested.

"Good call." I called out my familiar's name, and the little crow swooped over. "Can you go to the police station and see who's in there? Let me know."

"Of course, partner!" Jet zipped away while I joined Estelle in cleaning up tinsel and fallen pine leaves from Sylvester's tree. We didn't have many visitors today—most of the students had left swiftly following the tree incident—and I decided I should get on with something productive, like preparing for my next round of magical exams that I'd be taking in the new year.

I was on the fourth level of my magical studies, which was the most complex one yet, and while it was usually reserved for junior witches of around eleven years old, I'd had a delayed start to my magical education due to only moving into the library just over a year ago.

I needed to pick a specialist area to focus on for my studies, and when Estelle and I tried to brainstorm, we kept coming back around to my self-defence lessons against the vampires. I didn't think that was what *interested* me the most, though I couldn't deny that those skills were practical and had saved my life on more than one occasion.

"There's no way to incorporate them into an exam setting, though," I said. "I mean, they can't bring in a vampire to assess my skills at stopping someone from reading my thoughts." And as far as I knew, no spell or potion could grant that ability to a regular person.

"No, but you can focus on practical self-defence," she said. "Or theory, maybe. There's a lot of books on vampire history."

"I bet," I said. "I'm sure it's interesting, given that the vampires often write the history books themselves." Or they sent in corrections to the people who did. Sometimes they didn't seem to be able to help themselves. "I bet the Founders show up all over the place."

"They've been called various different names over the centuries," said Estelle. "But you don't have to make a research project of it if you don't want to. Pick something more pleasant."

"I don't know, it seems wise to know my enemy." My thoughts drifted to Evangeline. She wasn't the enemy, but an ally like her was one I'd keep at arm's length. "They're so… *tangled*. Like, that Victoire was friends with the Grim Reaper and apprenticed to two different Founders from different branches."

"She's still in Evangeline's jail?"

"I assume so. I didn't ask."

Evangeline generally arrested any rogue vampires herself, and to my knowledge, the dungeon's main current occupants were Victoire and Carlos Verdant, the other unpleasant Founder who'd concocted potions and experimented on humans in order to make various poisons that could kill even another vampire. That dungeon would also be Jaxon's inevitable fate if Evangeline found out about him.

"I hope Jaxon doesn't end up in there," I said. "Imagine how easily that information might make it back to the Founders if they ever escape."

"Would Evangeline let them, though?"

"No, but she also doesn't care that much about keeping the library's secrets. She's curious enough about us herself." As I'd been reminded on a not-infrequent basis ever since she'd learned of the existence of my dad's journal. "The annoying thing is that a vampire's mind-reading powers would really help us pin down the killer, but Jaxon can't do that." Could other vampires read *his* mind? Not a pleasant thought. At least there weren't many of those in jail unless Evangeline showed up, which was bound to happen eventually. Honestly, it was typical that he didn't have the one vampire power that we might actually need.

Except… wait. "We do know someone who can, though."

And someone who isn't entirely on Evangeline's side.

In other words—Laney.

6

I had to wait until sundown to speak to Laney. Work kept me busy, and I did make progress in nailing down some ideas for my next magical theory project between helping visitors track down the right books.

I was also making progress on translating my dad's journal, too, albeit in piecemeal sections. Dad had written the journal in a code that I'd had to translate one page at a time with the help of a magical contraption of his own creation, which was made more complicated by the number of out-of-order entries and digressions and after-the-fact interjections written in the margins that appeared all over the pages.

At lunchtime, Jet returned from the jail with the news that the police had invited in a group of witches to question but that he hadn't been able to get close enough to hear what they said. I didn't need the police berating me for sending my familiar to spy on their interrogations, so I was glad he'd kept his distance, but Aunt Adelaide called the jail and received a terse reply from Edwin saying that he hadn't been able to wake Jaxon from the deathlike sleep of a vampire. It didn't seem fair that the elf would have to stay at work late to finish the questioning, but even Aunt Candace couldn't control her fictional vampires' sleep schedules.

Aunt Candace herself came sauntering downstairs in the early evening, dressed as if she was going to a party.

"Where are you going?" Not the jail, surely. "I doubt Edwin's had time to question Jaxon yet."

"Oh, I'm not going there." She gave a laugh. "I intend to have a word with some of the karaoke club members."

"Edwin already questioned them, didn't he?"

"And you told me not to bother him. See? I can do as I'm asked."

Aunt Adelaide made a sceptical noise. "A karaoke night is hardly the right atmosphere to question anyone."

"Why do you think I'm going there early?" she enquired. "I happen to know some members of the club like to show up two or three hours beforehand to plan their song lists."

"But—" I broke off as she made for the door like a flowery whirlwind and disappeared out into the square. "They're not going to answer her questions. And even if they do, how's she going to avoid mentioning Jaxon isn't real? She even had to tell the police."

"Yes, and I gather that's presented a problem for Edwin," Aunt Adelaide said. "The law clearly puts the blame on Candace, should he be found guilty, but the library will certainly be drawn into the investigation as a consequence."

A yawn came from behind me, and Laney appeared in the doorway to the living quarters. "Hey, Rory. Anything new?"

Sometimes I envied her ability to sleep like the dead. "Jaxon got arrested as a murder suspect last night when someone showed up dead at karaoke night."

"Murder?" Her eyes widened. "A vampire death? I didn't hear about anything."

"Evangeline doesn't know." *Yet.* "Also, it might not have been him, but the victim's neck was broken, and since Jaxon found the body, it doesn't look good for him. Aunt Candace is convinced that he's innocent and has gone back to the pub to ask the other people who were there."

"Shouldn't that be the police's job?"

"I tried to tell her that, but Jaxon's been in a dead sleep all day and nobody has been able to question him, so she's getting antsy."

"Oh." She frowned. "I guess he was bound to draw suspicion even if he hadn't found the body."

"He also nearly started a fight with Edwin's guards because he felt threatened." I sighed. "It's not ideal. To top it off, the murder victim is one of the two witches I found trying to find the secret corridor yesterday, so it sounds like someone at the pub is spreading rumours about the library."

"No wonder your aunt went back there," she said. "I can always follow her and eavesdrop on a few people."

"I think the situation might call for it," I admitted. "But you really don't have to get involved if you don't want to."

"I know, but we *don't* want Evangeline involved, do we? And that's likely to happen the longer this goes unsolved."

She had a point. In fact, it wouldn't have surprised me if the vampires' leader had already become aware of the situation. She had no morals about reading the locals' minds herself, after all.

"You're going after Aunt Candace?" Estelle came into the lobby. "Oh, Laney… yeah, I can see where your abilities would come in handy."

I nodded. "Not sure it'll work, but someone needs to keep Aunt Candace out of trouble, if nothing else."

"Let me know how it goes."

We left the library for the Cocktail Cauldron, stepping out into the cold, rainy evening. Despite the weather—or maybe because of it—the pub was packed. Laney and I hovered in the doorway, scanning for Aunt Candace amid the crowd. Strangely, karaoke was already in progress, and the sound of someone warbling out of tune into a microphone drowned out all other noise.

"Is there karaoke *every* night?" asked Laney.

"Six nights a week, but I thought it didn't start for a few hours." I spied Aunt Candace talking to a tall wizard in the corner, her pen and notebook hovering at her side. "I don't know why they've started this early. It's barely six p.m."

Laney hung back, reluctant to enter the pub. "It's way too noisy in there for me to pick up anyone's thoughts."

"Oh." That was a downside to her vampire powers: over-sensitivity to noise. It also meant reading one person's individual thoughts would be a challenge. "Maybe you can wait outside?"

"Nah, I can handle it," she said. "At least I'm less likely to draw too much attention."

"There is that." I gave another glance over the crowd. "Ideally, I want to find Corrine, the witch who was with Patti when she showed up at the library, but I can't see her." I did see a few faces I recognised from the previous night, but the top-hat-wearing wizard Aunt Candace was talking to wasn't one of them.

"I'll do some snooping." Laney wove her way through the crowd with a vampire's grace. A few heads turned towards her, but most people were watching karaoke instead.

Aunt Candace narrowed her eyes when she saw me approaching her. "If you're here to drag me back to the library, you're wasting your time."

"I'm not. I'm here with Laney to find out who started that rumour about the library. Anyone catch your attention?"

"Are you now?" Her eyes gleamed. "You're finally putting that vampire friend of yours to good use?"

"She's not a mind-reading machine. Also, it's way too

noisy for her abilities to be fully effective in here. Why did they start karaoke this early?"

"It's a celebration of Patti's life, supposedly." She gave a snort. "If someone sings like that at *my* funeral, I'd rise from the dead just to make them stop."

"Aunt Candace," I hissed, hoping nobody else had heard her.

"What?" She grinned. "If there's anyone you want me to send your friend's way, let me know."

"Is there anyone here who you suspect?" I asked. "Who were you talking to just then?"

"Olli Greenfield," she said in disdainful tones. "One of Patti's friends."

"Any witches?" I scanned the group near karaoke, but it was hard to identify anyone from the back. Except for the female troll who towered over her companions as she put down her cocktail glass and climbed up onto the stage.

I braced myself to be thoroughly deafened and was instead taken off guard when the troll burst into an operatic song that was surprisingly tuneful, albeit as depressing as a funeral dirge.

"An opera-singing troll." Aunt Candace snorted. "That's a new one."

"I still have a hard time believing you and Jaxon came here voluntarily."

The troll had a decent voice, even when she burst into tears mid song and had to be led offstage by a group of friends. Including—*there she is.* I recognised Corrine among the group and kept an eye on her as I looked for Laney. I spied her standing by the bar, her pale face glowing with the light of a cocktail glass she held in her hand.

"This," she said in an undertone when I approached her, "is foul. It's like drinking concentrated sugar."

"I thought you didn't really go for human food anymore."

"No, but that guy at the bar was eyeing me suspiciously, so I figured I ought to buy something. He didn't even ask if I wanted blood, even to say they didn't have any."

I suppressed a shudder. A lot of pubs would serve a vampire if asked, though they were usually asked to provide their own sustenance unless the pub had a significant clientele of the fanged variety.

Seeing my expression, Laney held out her cocktail glass. "Want some of this?"

"Not particularly." I took the glass anyway and sniffed the contents then yelped when someone knocked into me from behind, causing me to spill the cocktail onto my shoes.

"Sorry!" the troll wailed, slumping onto a barstool, which sank beneath her with a loud creak. "I'm sorry."

"It's okay." I tried to reach for my wand to clean up, but someone else jostled me as more people took seats at the bar. My gaze snagged on Corrine, the witch from the library, who took a seat on the troll's other side, but the alarming creaking from the barstool warned that I was in danger of being crushed if I tried to walk behind her to reach the witch. My spine ached from where she'd knocked into me. A troll would certainly have the strength to inflict the blow that had killed Patti, but she and the witch had clearly been friends, and I had a hard time believing she'd ever hurt someone intentionally.

"I'm fine." I cut through her apologies, scrambling for a change of subject that would win me the chance to talk to her friend. "Ah, I liked your singing."

"Oh." She sniffed. "Thank you. It's not the same without her, you know?"

"Without Patti?" I guessed. "Yes, I heard she was a regular here."

Out of the corner of my eye I saw Laney move, shadowing the group from behind, and I found myself wondering if she could read a troll's mind as easily as a human's. I'd never had reason to ask before, but if she got close enough to the witches, she might be able to pick up on their thoughts, at least.

"Of course. She was here every night." She sniffed again, tears leaking from her eyes. "I miss her."

"We all do, Rhonda." The pink-haired witch leaned over and put an arm around her. "You gave her a great tribute."

"Thank you, Corrine." Rhonda sniffed again and called to the bartender, "Three more—and one for you as well?" she asked me.

"Erm, no thanks." I shifted uncomfortably as some of the other karaoke goers glanced curiously in my direction. "I'll just get a coke."

"They don't serve anything except cocktails." She eyed me blearily. "You're new here, aren't you?"

"Yeah. I'm here with my aunt." I'd rather they noticed Aunt Candace than Laney, who was currently lurking behind them. I wasn't sure where Aunt Candace was, but the karaoke stage appeared temporarily unoccupied, from what I could see. "They don't serve food." I was pretty hungry, actually, since this would usually be the time when I either went on a date with Xavier or had dinner with my family.

"What more do you need?" She took the glass from the bartender. It contained a bright-pink liquid that shimmered in rainbow colours when she held it up to the light, and she downed the whole thing in one go.

Laney had disappeared, so I excused myself and tried to approach Corrine from behind. The troll's stool chose that moment to collapse, tipping her onto the floor, and I slid sideways to avoid being crushed.

"I'm sorry!" she wailed again.

I scrambled to my feet and nearly fell over again when

half the bar's occupants stood up at the same time, all of them staring in anger and indignation at the karaoke area.

"What's she doing there?" Corrine, too, peered over the crowd. "I can't believe Trina would dare show her face here tonight."

"Is she?" Rhonda climbed upright, leaving a pile of splintered wood in place of the barstool.

I craned my neck, but the dense crowd made it difficult to see who they were staring at. "What's going on?"

"Trina," said Rhonda. "She and Patti weren't friends. It's downright insulting her showing up tonight when we're supposed to be celebrating Patti's life."

Hmm. "Was she here last night? Trina, I mean?"

"Of course. She's a regular. And not welcome here. Get out of here!" She raised her voice to a booming shout that was echoed throughout the crowd.

As the group from the bar moved towards the karaoke area, including the witch I'd been meaning to talk to, I tried to follow and slipped on the spilled cocktail. Only Laney's steadying hand on my shoulder kept me from falling flat on my face.

"Thanks." I caught my balance, whispering, "Find anything?"

Laney shook her head. "Reading drunk people's minds is slippery. And trolls are particularly hard, but that Rhonda isn't the killer, for sure."

"I didn't think so." I peered through a gap in the crowd and saw someone had placed a footstool on the stage, onto which an elf had climbed in order to reach the microphone. "That must be Trina."

"Who?"

"Someone who didn't like Patti." I watched the group from the bar move closer to the stage. "That witch—the one with the pink streak in her hair—is Patti's friend who was at the library."

"I'll try to get closer." She slipped through the crowd while I backed up against the bar before someone knocked me over again. There was a growing clamour near the stage when Patti's friends reached the elf's perch.

Laney listened for a minute and then returned to my side. "I heard Trina hated Patti's singing. Something about her always getting the lyrics wrong."

"That's what they're arguing about?"

"Only about Trina being here at all. They think it's disrespectful, but I didn't hear anything that pointed to her being the person they suspected of murder."

Hmm. Was bad singing a motive for murder? I mean, maybe. It was no less plausible than some of the alternatives, but that was up to Edwin to decide, and I somehow didn't think he'd be making arrests over someone mixing up song lyrics. There was a chance the police had already spoke to Trina and the others too.

"What about rumours about the library?" I asked. "You know, like Patti and her friend heard?"

"Nothing so far. I can try to get to Corrine again, but—"

The microphone screeched as the elf fell off the footstool into the crowd. Fists flew, and so did sparks, indicating someone had got out their wand.

"A brawl at karaoke. Now I've seen it all." I looked for the bartender, who was continuing to polish a glass, utterly oblivious to it all. I waved a hand to get his attention. "Excuse me."

"I'll get him." Laney skirted the bar and poked Shaw in the arm. He jumped a foot in the air, startled, but recovered when he saw the rowdy crowd. Reaching for his wand, he ducked out from behind the bar.

"Hey! Hey—stop it. My dad's gonna flip out if you wreck the place."

At first nobody heard him, but when he raised his voice, several people gasped. "We don't want to see Shaw Senior!"

Shaw's dad seemed to have a reputation, given how the crowd began to simmer down almost immediately. Shaw returned to his previous position at the bar, though he didn't cast another soundproofing charm, and I leaned over to talk to him. "Are you always left to handle all of them alone?"

"Like I said, our last assistant quit." He shrugged. "I don't mind, usually. They don't get rowdy that often."

"Still seems a lot for one person to handle." I could only assume he and his dad lived in the flat above, or else Shaw Senior was lurking in a back room somewhere. "Then you make all the cocktails yourself?"

With magic, I assumed. Given that every single person was drinking one, I was clearly in the minority in thinking they smelled way too sweet.

"They bring good business." Shaw shrugged again. "Anyway, if you're looking for your aunt, she already left."

"She what?" I hadn't seen, but she must have slipped outside during the ruckus. Scanning the room, I spied her hovering outside the front door.

Leaving the bar, I hastened to her side. "Why are you lurking outside?"

"I'm not lurking, I'm *loitering*," she said. "You're bright pink, did you know?"

I looked down at myself. Sure enough, my cloak had turned pinkish blue from the spilled cocktail. "You're avoiding the fight, aren't you? Or waiting to ambush Trina?"

"What would give you that idea?"

"The fact that everyone nearly started a fight with her because she and Patti hated each other so much."

"Exactly. She's obviously a contender for a suspect."

"It's Corrine I wanted to talk to." I looked around. "Where's Laney?"

"I imagine she went to talk to Evangeline."

My heart skipped a beat. "What?"

"You should've used a soundproofing spell if you've damaged your hearing from that racket."

"You know I heard you. I just wanted significantly more of an explanation for *why* you think Laney went to Evangeline. You know, the one person we *don't* want to know that there's a strange vampire in town. Or that he's been locked up as a murder suspect."

"I know because I saw them leave, of course," she said. "Just a minute ago."

"You might have told me sooner." *Oh no.* "Where'd they go?"

"I believe they went that way." She pointed downhill towards the square. "Laney did not look pleased."

I bet. "I'll find them. Please don't accuse anyone of murder while I'm gone."

I took off at a run down the darkened high street. The absence of any noise made it easy to spot the two vampires conversing near the square. At least they hadn't gone into the library or the police station, but why did Evangeline always have the absolute worst sense of timing? Had she *followed* Laney here?

"Ah, Aurora." Evangeline smiled at me, displaying her fangs. "Just the person I wanted to see."

The feeling isn't mutual, believe me. I clamped down on those thoughts, but her smile widened, enhancing her features. Yet there was a sinister edge to her beauty, her pale features too perfect, her hair too glossy to belong to the same world as the rest of us.

Laney had gone tense, her shoulders tight. "Leave Rory out of this."

"Out of what?" I looked between them. "What's this about?"

The vampires' leader had evidently found out *something*, but I didn't know if she was aware that my aunt had summoned a fictional vampire, that he'd been arrested, or everything else in between.

"Now, I believe it's more her business than yours," Evangeline reprimanded her. "Rory's aunt's actions affect the rest of her family, do they not?"

At her searching gaze, I tried to keep my mind blank, but the volume of noise from earlier had crept into my head and made it hard to judge how much I'd given away in the brief time we'd made eye contact.

"It certainly isn't *your* business," Laney retaliated. "Don't you even think of manipulating Rory."

"I'm doing nothing of the sort," she said. "Moreover, I believe this is very much my business. I understand that a new vampire is currently present in town who has been arrested as a suspect in a murder. Am I correct?"

"Not exactly." I backtracked. "Yes, he's a vampire, but he's not the same type of vampire as you are. He's fictional."

"Interesting," she said. "*Very* interesting. I would quite like to meet him."

"He's in jail—and that wasn't an invitation to disturb Edwin either," I added. "Jaxon's not one of your people. He's not accountable to the other vampires, and as soon as this is wrapped up, we'll send him back where he came from."

"Will you?" She smiled. "That library of yours is remarkable, isn't it? Might I ask how your aunt was able to accomplish such a feat?"

"The same as the last time," I evaded. "You know, when we had knights on horseback and monsters running all over the place about a year ago. Aunt Candace is the one who created him. She knows more than I do."

"Perhaps I will speak to her."

"If you do, I can't promise she'll answer." She wouldn't thank me for sending Evangeline after her, but it might stop her attempts to ambush Trina on the way out of the pub. Not to mention going back to the prison. While I did want to know if Edwin had managed to question Jaxon yet, Edwin didn't deserve to deal with all of us showing up at the station at night, especially the leader of the vampires. *Why now?*

Evangeline offered another smile. "Thank you for that insight, Aurora. I shall speak to her."

And in a blink, she was gone.

"So much for her not getting involved," I muttered to Laney. "Dammit."

"Sorry," Laney said. "She was hanging around outside the pub, so I went to see what she was up to. I shouldn't have come. I bet she followed me."

"It's not your fault. It's hers. She has to poke her nose into everything."

She sighed. "I guess if I were in her place, I'd probably be curious too."

"Tell me about it," I said. "I hope I satisfied her curiosity enough to leave well enough alone. She didn't even ask about the murder."

Which was weird, now that I thought about it. It was natural that Jaxon's presence would be of more interest to her than his arrest, but Evangeline must care about a vampire being accused of murder, even a fictional one. Right?

7

My initial plan was to go back to the library right away, but Aunt Candace shook off Evangeline quicker than I'd expected and caught us up halfway across the square.

She pointed an accusing finger at me. "You set the vampires on me, didn't you?"

"Evangeline came after me and Laney first," I said. "And you must have guessed she'd find out and take an interest in this. What did you say to get rid of her?"

"Surprisingly little," she replied. "I think she was more interested in snooping around the pub and breaking into a few minds along the way."

"She won't get much from them," Laney said. "Most are too drunk to make much sense. Those cocktails are potent."

"Looks like Rory is wearing one," said Aunt Candace with a laugh. "She's even glowing in the dark."

I flushed as brightly as the cocktail. "I wish I knew what tipped Evangeline off. I know she's got a habit of sticking her nose into any situation I'm involved in, but still."

Aunt Candace tutted. "Well, thanks to her, I never got the chance to speak to Trina."

"You mean accuse her of murder," I said. "Would that have got you anywhere? Really?"

"I wouldn't know now, would I?" she said. "As it is, I assume you at least prevented Evangeline from learning of Jaxon's origin?"

"I told her the same story we gave Edwin," I replied. "You know, that he came out of a book and that it was like that Manifestation Curse last year. She didn't seem interested in the actual murder."

"Oh, she is." Aunt Candace turned away as though to head to the seafront.

"Where are you going?" I asked. "Not the police station."

"Where else?" she said. "Edwin claimed he'd question Jaxon after sundown, and I intend to hold him to his word."

"It's late," I protested. "It's not fair of you to bother him after hours, especially after yesterday."

"I've been good and offered him more than enough time to finish his questioning, and I'd quite like for him to be let out of the holding cells before Evangeline inevitably pays him a visit."

That did seem to be a danger, I'd admit. "Do you really think Edwin will let Jaxon go? He doesn't have any other suspects, does he?"

"He might," she said. "Stop looking at me like that, Rory. If I was harbouring a killer, I would have asked the library to be rid of him right away. I'm not *that* attached to my fictional characters."

"Whether he's innocent or not, he's not acting like it, unless Edwin learned something suspicious from one of the other karaoke club members."

I wasn't sure if she was being truthful, but she might have been less affected by his vampire powers after being away from him all day. Which meant going back to the police station would likely bring her straight back under his influence, deliberate or not, but it couldn't be helped. I was still covered in sticky cocktail residue and in dire need of a shower, but I wouldn't let her go to the police station without one of us being present.

At least I had Laney with me for moral support, though she insisted on waiting outside so that Edwin wouldn't ask her too many questions.

When we entered the police station, Edwin sighed. "Let me guess. You were questioning people at the pub?"

"What a thing to accuse us of," said Aunt Candace.

"I'm covered in spilled cocktails," I reminded her. "Edwin, did you speak to Jaxon yet?"

"I did," he said. "He does claim to be innocent, but he was quite combative when I told him that you informed me that he came from a book."

"You weren't supposed to *tell* him that," said Aunt Candace. "May I talk to him?"

His eye twitched. "You may but only for five minutes."

He gestured, and one of the troll guards escorted her through the door into the jail. I watched, surprised he'd given in to her request that easily, but the poor guy looked as if he hadn't slept a wink the previous night.

"Did you talk to anyone else today?" I asked. "From karaoke, I mean? Patti had a lot of friends, but there were also people she disliked." One person—or elf—anyway.

"Nobody admitted to anything," he said. "By all accounts, she tripped and fell while drunk."

"Over a flat surface," I added. "Even if she did, breaking your neck is unlikely to happen by accident, isn't it?"

"The reports from the hospital confirmed that appears to be what occurred," he said. "There were no other wounds on her body, including bite marks."

"Xavier said the same," I admitted. "You should also know that Evangeline showed up at the pub tonight. She's taken an interest."

His eye twitched. "You drew her attention?"

"Not intentionally," I said. "She probably learned what was going on from reading someone's thoughts. She does that."

"That's…" He glanced over his shoulder at the jail. "I've made allowances for your family, but this situation puts me in a difficult position."

"I know, and I'm sorry," I said. "I think it'll cause you less hassle if he's not here, though. Did he really say anything that would implicate him in Patti's death?"

"No," he said. "While his explanation is… odd, I grant that he's no more likely to have committed the murder than anyone else who was present that night."

I was less convinced, but I had an inkling that Edwin wanted to avoid a visit from Evangeline, and who could blame him? "Then you're letting him go?"

"Regrettably, yes."

And just like that, Jaxon was free to come back to the library. Aunt Candace let out a loud squeal at the news and came out of the jail arm in arm with the vampire. He didn't look overly thrilled at walking free, but from what I'd read of his character, he probably considered it a grave insult that he'd been imprisoned in the first place.

Laney raised an eyebrow when we walked out of the police station. "Edwin let him go?"

"Yeah, I think he wanted to avoid a certain head vampire." So did I, and now we had to face the conundrum of what to do about a living fictional character roaming around town. My aunt seemed to have no intention of sending him back where he belonged, and it came as no surprise when they veered up the high street instead of towards the library.

"Where are you going?" I asked. "Please not back to karaoke night."

"Jaxon hasn't had a proper tour of the town yet," she said. "And no, we're not going back there, but you can't stop us from having any fun."

I knew when I was beaten. "Fine, but please try not to get into trouble."

As they departed, Laney gave a low whistle. "She's completely smitten, isn't she?"

"He has some influence over her," I explained. "Kind of like hypnosis, I guess. He can make anyone believe any word he says."

"She must have some level of resistance, being his creator, though."

"She might, but she's also biased for the same reason." Resigned, I turned back towards the library. "I hope they don't run into Evangeline."

It didn't sound like she'd been to the police station, but even if she and Aunt Candace didn't encounter one another tonight, it was only a matter of time before she came to the library asking to speak to the new vampire.

"I can keep an eye on them from a distance."

"No," I said. "No, we'll leave them to it. You don't have to spend any more of your time chasing them around."

Laney and I stopped to buy fish and chips from the local takeaway on the way back to the library and picked a spot in the Reading Corner to sit and eat. I was reminded of our childhood sleepovers when we'd been younger in Laney's cosy attic room. The floating lanterns coupled with the lights on Sylvester's Christmas tree—unlike the other tree, his was fully outfitted and not so much as a bauble had fallen off— made for a cosy atmosphere that banished some of my lingering unease.

Not all of it, though. After all, we now had an actual

fictional character living in the library... and Evangeline knew he was here.

————

I woke the next morning to the sound of Sylvester singing carols at a pitch that would have put off even the most avid karaoke goer. I took a leaf out of Shaw's book and cast a soundproofing spell so I could get a bit more sleep, but my mind was now thoroughly wide awake. Giving up, I went downstairs to the kitchen. Aunt Adelaide and Estelle were both early risers, but there was no sign of Aunt Candace nor her vampire companion when I found Estelle making breakfast in the kitchen.

"Did those two ever come back last night?" I asked as I joined her.

"They did," she confirmed. "Very late. Isn't Aunt Candace supposed to be giving you a magic lesson today?"

"Technically." My aunt was an erratic teacher at the best of times, and I was generally better off when left to my own devices. "I think we're starting on potion making. If she doesn't come downstairs, I can just read the textbook instead."

"I can help," Estelle offered. "I miss teaching, so it's no bother. I was thinking of volunteering at the university, actually, if I can fit it in around work at the library."

"And organising social events too," I added. "You weren't thinking of doing another PhD as well?"

"Maybe." She gave a wry grin. "I know. Cass called me a weirdo when I suggested it."

"So am I," I reminded her. "I would do a lot more studying if things didn't keep blowing up. I've spent longer rereading Aunt Candace's books this week than textbooks."

Let alone my dad's sorely neglected journal. I was starting

to think I'd need to exile myself to a desert island to finish the translation.

Estelle and I were finishing up breakfast when Aunt Candace came sailing into the kitchen wearing a wide smile. "It's a lovely day, isn't it?"

"Where'd you end up going last night?" I asked her.

"Around," she answered cryptically. "Relax, Rory. I didn't set foot in the Cocktail Cauldron."

Hmm. "Where's Jaxon?"

"Sleeping, of course. I procured him a coffin and a guest room."

"And then you're going to get rid of him. Right?"

"We've hardly got to spend any time together," she said indignantly. "You aren't willing to give him a chance; that's your problem."

"You were out all night, weren't you?" Estelle said. "You've had plenty of time."

Yeah, she's definitely under his spell again. Could we banish Jaxon without her input now that he was back in the library? If so, we'd probably have to carry the coffin up to the fourth floor, which was not ideal.

"You're just jealous."

"We really aren't," I said. "Come on. Can you think of the long-term consequences of summoning a fictional character? It's not like he can stay long-term."

"I don't see why not."

"The longer he stays, the more likely it is that people will figure out where he came from," I said. "Evangeline is already suspicious."

"Yes, and don't think I've forgotten you sent her after me last night."

"Because she showed up asking questions about the new vampire in town," I said. "I had to tell her he was fictional so she wouldn't try to recruit him to join her. Or try to kill him as a rogue."

"Aunt Candace, you know this reflects badly on the library as a whole," said Estelle. "At least consider listening to us. He can't stay forever."

"I never said he would," she said. "Also, anyone else who had access to a room like ours would do the same as I did. I can guarantee it."

"That doesn't mean conjuring up a fictional character is a sensible choice," I said. "Even without the murder. Also, what if he doesn't *want* to stay? He's been dragged away from his home."

"He has complete control over his free will, Rory. I'm not a monster."

Yes, but does he have control over your *free will?* More to the point, had he exercised that same free will to commit murder?

Aunt Candace gave an exaggerated yawn. "I think I will have a nap."

"And not give Rory her magic lesson?" Estelle gave her a pointed look.

"It's fine." I could only imagine what kind of nonsense she'd end up lecturing me about if I let her take over my lesson as usual. "I can read the textbook."

"You did promise my mother," Estelle said to Aunt Candace. "It won't kill you to supervise her. Jaxon's sleeping, so you don't have anything else to do."

My aunt gave a sigh. "If you insist."

We made for the classrooms at the back of the ground floor, having to skirt around both Christmas trees on the way and duck a shower of tinsel that was probably Sylvester's doing. He sometimes came to supervise my lessons and offer unhelpful advice, but he didn't emerge from the tree as we walked past. At least he'd stopped singing.

I tended to prefer theory lessons to practical ones, as Aunt Candace usually sat in the corner reading while I brewed potions or practised spells and then tried to get her attention for long enough to get meaningful feedback. Potions were particularly hands-on as far as topics went, and when I opened the textbook and found that I was supposed to start studying poisons, Aunt Candace suddenly took an interest.

"Ah, my favourite topic," she said. "So many interesting ways to kill people."

"Have you used them all in your books?"

"Not yet." She waved her wand, and a set of ingredients appeared in front of me. "Identify the poisons and their effects. I assume you already read that chapter?"

"I did." She hadn't known that for sure, but I wasn't complaining about being given something a bit more advanced. I hadn't forgotten the time she'd made me spend ages cutting up yarrow roots. "I don't have to brew an actual poison in the exam, do I?"

"Oh yes." She grinned. "Occasionally students try to use it on the examiner. That's always memorable. Oh, and you might want to take off your cloak. Those poisons can leave traces on your clothes."

I did so, and then I got on with sorting out the plants and herbs into various piles and noting their effects. The potent smell was uncomfortably reminiscent of the lab I'd found at the Founders' hideout, which had been full of their sickening attempts to experiment on humans to develop potions that had various effects on vampires. For that reason alone, I was glad Carlos Verdant was safely behind bars and that the sole known copy of the recipe for a poison capable of stopping a vampire's heart was safe inside the library. I didn't know exactly how it'd ended up in the form of an untranslated document at the town's university that had led to several murders before we'd got it back into our own hands, but I suspected a connection with the Founders' attempts to recruit students from the university to join their cause and turn them into vampire lab rats.

They'd targeted normals, too, which was how Laney had been turned into a vampire in the first place. She'd barely begun to adjust when she'd been hit by the same poison and had nearly died, and I'd only been able to save her thanks to a phoenix feather conjured up by the fourth-floor corridor. That was the first and only time I'd used a wish from the corridor, and if you asked me, its original purpose was to handle emergency situations. Summoning fictional characters definitely didn't qualify as urgent, but I knew better than to pursue that line of argument with Aunt Candace.

When I'd finished sorting the poisons, I got her attention, and she checked my work. "Perfect, obviously."

"Thanks." From her, that was high praise. "Anything else? I peeked at the next chapter, and…"

"Meaning you already read it." She rolled her eyes at me. "And you accuse *me* of needing a better hobby."

I ignored the jibe. I'd been interested when I'd found part of the chapter covered potions that affected someone's mental state, including subtle persuasion and influence. No cure was mentioned, but I had to wonder if there might be a potion that could erase the spell Aunt Candace's vampire friend had exerted over her.

"I think we're done here." She walked to the door. "Oh, and you might want to have a shower and avoid touching any food for a bit if you want to avoid poisoning anyone. Though that boyfriend of yours might survive it since he's already dead."

"He's not dead." She had a point, though. "I'll go and clean up."

I scrubbed myself thoroughly in the shower and left my clothes with the outfit that had got soaked in cocktails the previous day in the laundry basket. Then I returned downstairs to help the others open the library for the day. With Jaxon sleeping, we could almost pretend to return to normality, and when no visitors entered at first, I pulled out the textbook again.

"Was Aunt Candace no help in your lesson?" Estelle asked, seeing what I was reading.

"No, she was fine," I replied. "I'm wondering if there's an anti-mind-control potion we can brew. One that can remove influences over someone's mind."

"What—oh. Like the vampire's abilities?"

"Yeah," I said. "I don't know if there's anything that'll work on someone who's under a spell that isn't even from the same version of reality as ours, though."

"Good thinking." She nodded slowly. "That won't be in the textbook for Grade Four, but you might find something more specialist in the Potions and Poisons Section."

"I thought so." I resolved to check when I had a spare moment, though as it was another rainy day, we soon drew in a stream of visitors who'd come to take refuge. Estelle and I received a lot of compliments on the decorations, though the two giant Christmas trees did make it difficult to retrieve books from the ground floor.

When I had a spare moment, I waylaid Aunt Adelaide. "Hey. I wondered, might it be possible to use a potion to cure the vampire's mind-altering effect on Aunt Candace?"

"Oh, that's a good point," she said. "A potion might do the trick. I don't think that vampire's spell is going to wear off her otherwise without someone intervening."

"That's what I thought," I said. "It'll be in the Potions and Poisons Section."

"Yes, but those potions are a bit advanced." She pursed her lips. "Candace wouldn't be pleased with me for suggesting it."

"She doesn't want to be under his spell forever, does she?" I queried. "I'm not that keen on the idea either, but we need her to come to her senses before anything else happens."

Or before the police arrested him again. As far as I knew, they hadn't found the real killer, as Xavier told me when he showed up at lunchtime with a bag of goodies from the bakery.

"Sorry I didn't get in touch yesterday," he said to me. "My boss was being difficult. He kept asking questions about why Evangeline was hanging around that pub last night."

"He knew?" I asked. "I sent her packing, but I thought your boss didn't care about people being murdered as long as their souls ended up where they were supposed to."

"Usually not, but anything involving the vampires sets him on edge."

"He's not the only one." I took in a breath. "Did you tell him about Aunt Candace's friend?"

"No, I didn't. Wait. Did Jaxon get out of jail?"

"Last night." I filled him in on what he missed. "I think Edwin only let him out to avoid a chat with Evangeline. I'm not convinced she'll stay away from the library for long. She's fascinated by Jaxon."

"At least he isn't wanted for murder anymore," he said. "Want to go out tonight?"

"Definitely." We were long overdue a date *without* any Reaper-related interruptions.

Famous last words, Rory.

8

As the sky outside darkened, the clamour of noise upstairs indicated the resident vampires were awake. Jaxon and Aunt Candace walked out of the living quarters first, arm in arm.

"Where are you going?" I asked.

"Out," Aunt Candace answered. "The night is young, and the possibilities are endless."

As they departed, Estelle groaned softly. "Not again."

"Someone has to watch them." I called for my familiar. "Jet, can you follow Aunt Candace? Try not to let her see you —and Jaxon too."

"Of course, partner!" He took off, soaring out of the open door.

"I didn't expect them to leave this early." It was barely four thirty in the afternoon, and the library hadn't closed yet. We'd had so many visitors that I hadn't been able to spend more than a few minutes up in the Potions and Poisons Division, not long enough to track down any concoction that might help us lift the vampire's spell. "So much for curing her of his influence."

"A potion would have taken a few days to brew," she said. "We still have time."

"Unless…" The obvious hit me. "I bet the fourth-floor corridor can conjure up a cure."

"There's still time to try," she agreed. "Though we'd need to ensure Aunt Candace actually drinks it."

"Drinks what?" Aunt Adelaide walked into view. "Don't tell me that was my sister."

"They went on a walking tour," I said. "Or something like it. We were discussing using the fourth-floor room to conjure up a potion to break the vampire's spell on Aunt Candace. It's quicker than brewing a cure ourselves."

"But riskier," she said. "I would say that using the room to banish him would be more effective, but my sister would likely never forgive us if we went behind her back. It also might not work for us. There's a possibility that only the person who conjured him up can banish him."

"Then we'd have to bring her to her senses," I said. "I know it's not ideal. Sylvester warned me off the last time I thought about using that room to make a wish."

"Ask him," she suggested. "Or ask the Book of Questions."

"I should have asked sooner, really." I peered behind the desk and saw that Aunt Candace had returned the book to its former spot.

Picking up the Book of Questions, I flipped it open. "I wish to enter—"

The door opened, and Jet flew back into the library, shrieking, "Danger! Danger!"

"Oh, god." I closed the book. "What is it this time?"

"The vampires are fighting!" he squeaked.

"Which vampires?" Not *Evangeline*. I dropped the Book of Questions on the desk and ran out of the library. Drizzle blew into my face, and the cold breeze cut through my cloak to my skin as I turned up the high street and ran until I reached the renovated church where the vampires made their home. Its spired roof looked spookier than ever in the cold rain, silhouetted against the darkening sky, and outside, Jaxon stood face-to-face with Evangeline, his fangs out and his posture readied for a fight. Evangeline's stance was more casual, but I saw the predator lurking beneath her pretty face.

Gasping for breath, I halted at Aunt Candace's side. "What's going on?"

She didn't answer. Her attention was riveted on the others as the vampires stared each other down.

"Aunt Candace, you didn't bring him *here*, did you?" I whispered to her.

"He came here himself," she muttered back. "I couldn't stop him."

"Aurora," said Evangeline without so much as a glance at me, "I would prefer to deal with this rogue vampire myself."

"He's not a rogue," I said. "I told you, he's not local. He's not even from this *planet*."

"He should not have set foot near my territory." She bared her teeth, and Jaxon hissed right back at her. "You should know from living in the library that a person created by a curse is just as dangerous as their living counterpart."

"What is that supposed to mean?" Jaxon snarled.

"I assumed your creator would have told you about your origin," said Evangeline. "Perhaps you ought to discuss the matter between yourselves."

And she vanished back into the house, the oak doors closing behind her with a soft thud. Jaxon's gaze remained fixed on the closed door, a snarl slipping between his teeth. "How dare she?"

"It's better to leave her alone," I told him. "Trust me."

Aunt Candace shifted on her feet. "Come on, Jaxon. Ignore her."

"She insulted me," growled the vampire. "She said I was cursed."

"She said a curse created you." I tried to catch Aunt Candace's eye. "Which is true. Right, Aunt Candace?"

My aunt ignored me. "She's jealous, nothing more. You have abilities that the other vampires don't."

"Aunt Candace." I moved closer and whispered, "You didn't tell him he came out of a book?"

"I came from where?" Jaxon turned to me, shock rippling across his face. "You're lying."

My mouth parted. I'd forgotten his super senses would pick up on my words, but I'd assumed my aunt had already given him the full story.

Jaxon's gaze slid between us, and then, in a blur of movement, he was gone.

"Thanks for that, Rory." Aunt Candace marched after him, leaving me staring at Evangeline's closed door. *Dammit.* Why had she brought him here?

I hesitated for a moment then turned back down the high street. I was halfway to the library when I heard my name.

"Rory?"

I halted, seeing Xavier peering over the fence to the cemetery. "What's going on? Were you at the vampires' house?"

"Aunt Candace," I explained. "Jaxon decided to trespass on Evangeline's territory. It went about as well as you'd think."

His eyes widened. "They got into a fight?"

"Almost, until I accidentally told him he wasn't real and that he came out of a book," I said. "Turns out my aunt never told him, and I think the truth sent him into an existential crisis."

"Then he's gone?"

"He ran off, and my aunt followed him." I took in a breath. "I'll tell you more when we're back at the library."

We walked the rest of the way to the library, and I opened the front door. "Honestly, what did Aunt Candace expect when she brought him outside? Of course he'd be curious about the other vampires."

"Hey, Xavier," Estelle said to him. "What was Jet yelling about?"

"Jaxon had a standoff with Evangeline," I replied. "He decided to get too close to her territory. Then he took off when I told him he actually came out of a book. I didn't realise Aunt Candace neglected to tell him."

"Oh no." She winced. "Did she go after him?"

I nodded. "I hope he didn't leave town. She's still under his spell, and if she leaves, there's no guarantee either of them will come back."

"Under his spell?" asked Xavier.

"The vampires in her series have the ability to influence others' thoughts," I clarified. "He might not even realise he's doing it, but Aunt Candace isn't acting under her own power. I know I should have gone after her, but I'm not sure I'd have been able to convince her to turn back."

"Probably not." Estelle's expression darkened. "This is a problem."

"Tell me about it," I said. "I knew I should have found a way to undo that spell. I was about to ask Sylvester before I got distracted when Jet called me out of the library."

"Want to do it now?" Xavier suggested. "Otherwise, I can track your aunt using my Reaper abilities if you want me to."

"Best save that for a last resort." I reached for the Book of Questions, which I'd placed on the desk. "I wish to enter the Forbidden—"

"Rory." Xavier's eyes went wide. "I'm being called to pick up a—"

The room swallowed me up before I could hear the rest,

and I toppled headfirst into the pages. I landed on my back, Xavier's words echoing in my ears.

There was only one possible end to that sentence. *Soul.* Which meant someone else was dead.

I sat upright, my mind reeling. The room was free of decorations and back to its usual blank-walled state.

"Going to ask a question?" asked a disembodied voice.

"Yes." I marshalled my thoughts the best I could. I'd learned that starting a question with *can you* would get me an unhelpful monosyllabic answer in exchange, so I asked, "Will you give me a book containing a recipe for a potion to erase the effects of mind control?"

"You'll have to be more specific. There's a large number of mind-control spells."

"I don't know if this counts as a spell," I said, "since it's cast by a fictional character who isn't even from the same reality as we are. But it's all I've got."

A thump sounded as a book fell out of the sky, landing in front of me. I picked it up, reading the faded title. *Potions of the Mind.*

"And I'll give you this advice for free," said Sylvester's voice. "With a spell such as the one your aunt used to conjure that vampire into being, everything depends upon your aunt's belief in her own creation. As long as that persists, there'll be no getting rid of him."

"As long as…" Wait a moment. "You mean we can't use the upstairs corridor to banish him. Aunt Candace has to do it herself."

In answer, the room tipped over, and I tumbled out, landing on my back next to the desk.

Estelle peered down at me. "Oh—Rory. Sorry. Xavier left. He…"

"He said he'd been called to collect a soul?"

She inclined her head. "Yes. I don't know who it was."

"I'll find him." I rose upright, finding that the book the room had given me had landed at my side. *Potions of the Mind.* Resolving to check it for recipes later, I left the book on the desk and ran out of the library.

What are the odds that Jaxon was involved? The thought nagged at me as I walked, and a curtain of rain swept down on my head. Huddled inside my cloak, I ran across the square and spied Aunt Candace coming the other way. "Hey, wait."

"What?" she asked. "Haven't you done enough damage?"

She's under a spell, I reminded myself. "Someone's dead. Xavier was called to collect a soul. Did you see him?"

"No, I didn't." She rotated on her heel. "Where?"

"I don't know." When in Reaper mode, he could walk past someone in broad daylight and not be seen—but *I* could see him, and when I saw Edwin emerge from the seafront with two troll guards in tow, I veered towards them.

"Aurora," he said. "If you wanted to see me, you'll have to wait."

"That's not it," I said. "I was going to find Xavier, and I assumed you were heading the same way."

His eyes narrowed. "I was called to the scene of an attack, but I'd prefer for the pair of you to stay out of this. Unless your resident vampire is perhaps implicated?"

Aunt Candace joined me, her pen and notebook somehow not absorbing so much as a drop of rainwater as they hovered at her side. "Certainly *not.* Thanks to my niece, he's not even here."

"You think he left town?" I didn't want to implicate Jaxon in the crime so soon after his release, but without the facts, I couldn't begin to guess what had happened. "Ah, do you know *who* was attacked? And where? I just want to find Xavier."

Edwin stepped around my aunt and strode across the square. "I'm sure he'll find his way to you without my input."

"It's not near the Cocktail Cauldron, is it?" I knew that my aunt's presence wouldn't help matters, but I didn't want to let her out of my sight either.

When we reached the high street, I spied Xavier coming the other way.

"Rory." He hurried to join me. "Sorry I ran off."

"Who died?" Aunt Candace asked. "Do tell."

For once, Xavier's expression was almost as grim as his boss's. "A wizard named Olli. He… He was killed by a vampire."

"It was a vampire attack?" My heart plummeted. "Where?"

"Up there." He pointed uphill. "Not on Evangeline's territory but close enough to have me worried. I don't think either of you should go there."

"I'll make that decision," Aunt Candace said. "Unless you'd like to speak to the police yourself and report back to us, Reaper."

"That's not Xavier's job." Admittedly, I was curious enough myself, but that didn't mean I wanted Xavier to end up at a crime scene instead of on a date with me.

"My boss will want me to report in," he said apologetically. "Deaths inflicted by vampires always catch his attention, even if there's no chance of the person coming back to life."

"Isn't there?" I asked. "The attack wasn't intended to turn him into a vampire?"

He shook his head. "There were bite marks but shallow ones. I'm not sure what the actual cause of death was."

"How disappointing," said Aunt Candace. "I think I shall have a closer look myself."

"Edwin won't let you," I replied. "You know that. I thought you wanted to find Jaxon anyway. Do you really think he left town?"

"You hope so, don't you?" She glared at me, the effect

somewhat dampened—literally—by the rain plastering her hair to her forehead. "You'll never understand what exists between us."

"Right." If she wanted to get herself into trouble with the police again, there was little I could do to stop her, but I couldn't help wondering where Jaxon was hiding. "Xavier…"

"I'm sorry, Rory." He drew me into a hug. "We can reschedule our date for tomorrow. And I can try to stop by later, if my boss lets me."

"Or if nobody gets arrested again." I spoke in a low voice, conscious of my aunt within hearing distance. Really, I was less upset about missing our date than I was about, well, everything else. "I'll tell the others."

As little as I wanted to leave her at a crime scene unsupervised, Edwin's presence would make her less likely to cause trouble, at least for a bit. I walked back to the library, where all my remaining family members had gathered in the lobby, even Cass. She must have come downstairs when she'd heard the noise, or else one of the others had fetched her.

"You look like a drowned rat," said Cass. "Don't tell me Aunt Candace got arrested again. Or Jaxon did."

I cast a drying spell on my sopping wet hair and cloak. "No, he's missing, and someone else is dead in a suspected vampire attack."

Aunt Adelaide hissed out a breath. "This has gone too far. He has to go."

"He's already gone," I said. "That's the problem. He ran off, and you know how fast vampires move."

"He left town?" Estelle asked.

"I don't know." I almost hoped he had. "Not sure where he'd go, though."

"He can't have left town," said Aunt Adelaide. "I didn't mention this earlier, but a creation of a Manifestation Curse is usually tied to its source. The same likely applies to him."

My mouth fell open. "Does that mean he'll disappear if he goes too far from the library? He'll just cease to exist?"

"Yes," she said. "Don't forget even our magic is less effective away from the library."

That was true, though it didn't stop working altogether. "And you think he's aware of that?"

"If not, we're finally rid of him," said Cass. "Good riddance."

"He'll be aware," said Aunt Adelaide darkly. "Through subconscious instinct, if nothing else. Is my sister looking for him?"

"She was, and then she went to the crime scene instead."

"Of course she has," Cass said. "What's with the potion book?"

"This?" I picked up the book I'd left on the desk. "I got it from the Forbidden Room. I was looking for a cure for the vampire's hold over Aunt Candace. I think Aunt Candace is the only one who can get rid of him permanently."

Aunt Adelaide swore under her breath. "I was afraid of that."

"Anyway, Aunt Candace is at the crime scene trying to find out who the victim was. A wizard, Xavier said."

"Victim?" Laney appeared in the doorway to the living quarters. "What? Not another murder?"

"A vampire committed this one."

The remaining colour drained from Laney's face. "Oh no."

"Exactly."

9

fter I told Laney the rest of what she'd missed while she'd been sleeping, she offered to go to look for Jaxon herself. "I can move quickly enough to cover the whole town. Might be able to find your aunt too."

"I know where she is. Unfortunately." I grimaced. "Pestering Edwin at a crime scene. Jaxon, though, I have no idea."

"Really, there are only a few places he might be hiding out," said Laney. "One of which is, well, the vampires' place."

"Evangeline already kicked him out," I said, though she was unpredictable at the best of times. "I wouldn't have thought he'd have gone to her after what she said to him earlier, but she'll also be in a foul mood if she finds out a vampire killed someone."

Which offered another concerning point—namely, that if Jaxon *wasn't* the killer, did that mean there was a rogue vampire in town?

Dammit. If Evangeline was roaming around, I didn't want Laney to end up being ambushed again. Nor Aunt Candace, come to that.

"You're not going out again?" Estelle guessed, seeing the look on my face.

"I don't *want* to, but Evangeline is guaranteed to be livid when she finds out that a vampire committed a murder, whether it was one of her people or not. I don't want Laney or Aunt Candace to end up in the firing line."

"Good point." Aunt Adelaide's expression darkened. "All right, but come back right away if there's trouble."

There almost certainly will be. Evangeline might not know there'd been a vampire-related death yet, but rescuing Aunt Candace would have to come before finding Jaxon. Whether she *wanted* to be rescued was another matter entirely.

"I shouldn't have let her go to the crime scene in the first place," I said. "I completely forgot Evangeline would be first on the scene when she finds out it's a vampire killing. I'm not even sure where exactly the death took place."

"I'll find them." Laney glided ahead of me out of the library, angling towards the high street and the route to the vampires' house. It was fully dark by now, and my heart skittered when I glanced over the fence at the cemetery. The high street was generally well lit, but all light seemed to flee that area, as though chased off by the Grim Reaper himself. I hoped he wouldn't give Xavier too much of a hard time when he reported the vampire-inflicted death.

A similar darkness cloaked the vampires' home, and my skin prickled. Nothing good came from visiting the vampires after dark, let alone when one of them might have committed murder.

Laney trod ahead of me and halted outside. "Oh. There's your aunt."

"Aunt Candace." I spied her lurking below the window of the vampires' place. "What *are* you doing?"

"The same as you, presumably," she said. "I'm looking for Jaxon, and I'll thank you not to give me away."

"I can guarantee Evangeline has already noticed you. You do remember she and Jaxon nearly ripped each other to shreds less than an hour ago?"

"She's not here," she said. "She went to the vampires' school to teach her fanged children how to look creepy."

"I thought you were questioning Edwin at the crime scene." What on earth was she thinking? "Did Edwin send you packing?"

"He was quite rude to me." She tutted. "Poor Olli didn't deserve to die like that."

"Who was the victim?" I asked. "He wasn't part of the karaoke club, was he?"

"You might have seen me talking to a man wearing a top hat the other night."

My heart dropped like a stone. "Oh no."

"You do realise a vampire killed him, right?" Laney asked Aunt Candace. "And you're right outside their door. You must know Jaxon isn't here."

"Exactly." I peered over her shoulder at the window. The glass was covered in such a thick skein of cobwebs that it was difficult to see inside, but I did see a few figures moving around inside. Even if Evangeline wasn't present, the other vampires would surely have noticed their visitor.

The front door opened, and another vampire peered out. She was as stunning as Evangeline, blond and delicate, and she eyed Aunt Candace like a tasty snack. "May I help you?"

"Have you taken in any new vampires recently?" she asked. "I seem to have lost mine."

I groaned inwardly. The vampire studied her with a smile. "Ah, you mean the handsome newcomer?"

"Jaxon?" Aunt Candace flashed me a look saying *I told you so.*

"That's him," she said. "He's delightful, isn't he? So mysterious and intriguing."

"When… When did he get here?" I asked. "I thought Evangeline threw him out."

Unless… Oh no. He couldn't have used his abilities on *her*, could he?

"I'd like to talk to him," said Aunt Candace. "May I come in?"

"You'll have to ask our leader," said the vampire. "Ah, there she is."

I tensed when Evangeline herself came into view, her pretty face twisted in a scowl. Laney moved closer to me, though Aunt Candace remained near the door, craning her neck to see past the vampire.

"What a cosy gathering," Evangeline remarked. "Would one of you like to explain?"

My mouth parted. Did she not know Jaxon was here?

Aunt Candace leapt in. "I'd like to speak to Jaxon. Might I ask why you decided to invite him in?"

My body tensed even further and then relaxed marginally when she replied, "You may ask, but Jaxon himself will have to answer."

At least she actually knew he was in her home, but how long had he been there for? Had he entered before or after the murder? And did he have a hold over Evangeline? She didn't *look* as though she was under his spell, but the vampires' leader was impossible to read. Literally. "Why'd you let him into your home? I thought you didn't like him."

"We came to an understanding," she said. "After I caught him outside for the second time, I decided to offer him the option to shelter with the other vampires."

"And when was this?" I glanced at Aunt Candace, who glowered in the vampires' leader's direction.

"Perhaps half an hour ago," she said. "Have you satisfied your curiosity?"

"Not exactly," said Laney. "Also, didn't you hear a vampire murdered someone?"

Evangeline went from suspicious to predatory in a heartbeat. "No, I did not. Explain."

Her chilling tone brought a shiver of fear to my skin. "A wizard was found dead. He had bite marks on his neck, but that wasn't what killed him. I think Edwin is still at the crime scene. Right, Aunt Candace?"

She finally peeled her gaze away from the door. "I want to talk to Jaxon."

"If he's inside my home, I assume he doesn't want to talk to you," Evangeline said. "I will speak to Edwin myself."

Harsh. I didn't know if she was right, but I'd also thought she didn't consider Jaxon to be one of her fellow vampires. Even if she hadn't known of the more recent murder, did she not care that he might have been responsible for Patti's death?

She turned her back and glided down the nearby street. I hurried after her, and Laney swiftly overtook me. Though Aunt Candace didn't follow, her notebook and pen floated after us of their own accord, and both came to an abrupt halt when we encountered Edwin coming the other way.

"Evangeline." He peered up at her, fear flickering across his face. "Ah, I intended to visit you—unless you have another appointment?"

"If you intended to visit me for the reason I suspect, no."

Oh boy.

He took in a breath. "Yes, I intended to inform you that someone was seemingly killed by a vampire, as you requested for me to let you know of any attacks involving one of your people."

"One of my people was *not* responsible for this." She bared her teeth. "Take me to the scene of the attack."

He shifted on his feet, uncomfortable. "The body has already been removed, but it's this way."

Evangeline glided after him, with Laney close behind her. As I made to follow, Edwin cleared his throat. "I don't recall offering you permission to go to the crime scene, too, Rory. Your aunt has already spent enough time hassling me."

"I'm sorry about her." I was too. "But if there's a rogue vampire in town, you know there's a chance that they might be after my family."

"Your aunt said the same." He paused. "You can come, then, but don't touch anything."

I didn't particularly *want* to walk to a murder scene, nor contemplate the possibility of another rogue in connection with the Founders being in the area. I didn't believe they were—the last ones I'd encountered were currently imprisoned in Evangeline's dungeon—but the alley in which the body had been found was within a minute's walk of their home.

I hung back, not wanting to get too close to the scene. Evangeline stalked into the alleyway and sniffed at the air. Her super-attuned vampire senses would let her know if there *was* a rogue present, but the same went for Laney.

"Can you pick up on the killer's scent?" I asked her.

"Nope, only the victim and us," Laney said. "But I'm still learning how to make use of my vampire talents."

"Yes, and you've been neglecting your studies." Evangeline returned to her side. "Tell me what you smell."

"Blood, mostly," she said.

Nausea rolled over me. "I don't think we need to know anything else."

Evangeline ignored me. "And?"

Laney sniffed again. "Hmm. Smells like one of those cocktails."

"Had the man who died been at the pub earlier, do you

think? Or might it be from yesterday?" Come to think of it, if karaoke night started early again, some people might already be there.

There was one other possibility, of course: the person responsible for the murder had come from the pub.

I frowned at Evangeline. "You didn't come to that pub yesterday on a whim, did you?"

"No," she said, "I did not."

My heart skipped. "You knew… What did you know? The first murder wasn't committed by a vampire. Not in an obvious way."

I didn't need to spell out my suspicions about Jaxon's involvement, but I pulled on all the mind-reading-resisting skills I had at my disposal to keep my attention on the question of who'd been responsible for the murder and not on where Jaxon had truly come from.

"I have to say, I'm surprised that you didn't inform me of the incident sooner," she said. "I thought you had a higher sense of danger surrounding rogue vampires, Aurora."

"I didn't think the killer was a rogue." She was right. My experience with vampire rogues had chiefly involved them targeting me and me escaping by the skin of my teeth, but until the wizard's death, nothing in this situation had implied the Founders' potential involvement. With Aunt Candace still not around, I risked asking the question that was nudging at the forefront at my mind. "Are you sure Jaxon wasn't involved? Did you read his mind?"

"I cannot." A warning bite entered her voice. "His thoughts are impenetrable to me."

"You *can't* read his thoughts?" I gaped at her. "Seriously?"

"Yes," she said. "After all, he is not from the same world as we are."

I closed my mouth, my own thoughts spinning in circles.

"Then why let him into your home? You must know you can't trust him."

"To study him, of course." She gave me a piercing look. "Believe it or not, I am fully aware of the danger."

"I know, but"—I licked my dry lips—"he has mind powers too. He can subtly influence people. Does that have any effect on you?"

"I noticed no change," she said coldly. "Be careful, Aurora."

She vanished from the alleyway, disappearing like mist in the rain.

"I hope he's not affecting her mind," I murmured to Laney. "Really, I'm the one who should be giving *her* a warning, not the other way around."

"I can check," she said uncertainly. "She kinda had a point about me skipping out on lessons recently."

"Yes, because we don't need her knowing…" I trailed off, conscious that Edwin was nearby, too, and that he didn't know the full story of where Jaxon had come from either. "Also, we should probably get Aunt Candace away from the vampires' house."

"Good point." She glided out of the alley and joined me in leaving the murder scene behind. "It does smell of cocktails back there, a little."

"And Jaxon?" I asked. "Did you pick up on *his* scent?"

"I honestly don't know," she said. "Like I said, I'm not as attuned into these things as Evangeline is."

"No, but I don't think one of her vampires is responsible for this." Unless someone had wanted to frame the vampires on purpose, but who would do that, and why? Unfortunately, Jaxon remained at the top of the suspects list, and while it made some level of sense that Evangeline would want to keep him close at hand, that might spell trouble for Edwin. And us.

Aunt Candace remained where we'd left her, her gaze fixed on the closed door to the vampires' house. Evidently, Jaxon had not come out to talk to her.

"What are you doing?" I spied her notebook and pen, which must have returned to her side at some point. "Jaxon is with Evangeline now. It's probably for the best."

"You would say that," she said sourly. "She's bewitched him."

"If anything, it's the other way around." I dropped the subject when she gave me a warning stare. "Look, someone was just killed by a vampire. A vampire who recently set foot in a certain pub."

"Really?" Her gaze sharpened. "Interesting. Karaoke night will be kicking off in an hour or so."

"You want to go there." There was possibly nowhere I was *less* interested in going, but it might be worth asking some question to see if Olli had been there earlier—or Jaxon.

The pub was on the way back to the library regardless, and since I'd successfully diverted Aunt Candace's attention from the vampires, I had fewer qualms about letting her take a detour. Unlike the previous day, the Cocktail Cauldron wasn't that busy, and Laney immediately attracted a few puzzled glances when she entered. Some of Patti's friends sat at the bar, including Rhonda and Corrine. All of them were holding vibrant cocktails and had their heads bowed together in hushed conversation. Had they already heard about Olli's death? I kept an eye on Corrine as my aunt pulled out a stool and sat down next to the group, her pen and notebook bobbing up and down in the air behind her.

Laney hung back behind their group with a vampire's stealth, but Rhonda spotted my approach. "Oh, you're back here for karaoke? You didn't sing last time."

"Erm, someone started a fight, remember?" I might want

answers, but I drew the line at participating in karaoke in order to get them.

"Ah, because that Trina tried to get in on Patti's celebration." She scowled. "She only wanted the attention."

That reminded me. The elf didn't appear to be around today, but I could safely remove her from the suspects list for Olli's death. I had a hard time believing that an elf had killed someone with a vampire-style bite. I didn't think elves *could* become vampires, for that matter, and the same went for trolls. That also ruled out Rhonda as a suspect too.

"I bet." Aunt Candace jumped right in. "Olli was murdered earlier, did you know?"

"That's what we were talking about," said one of the others. "It's horrible, isn't it?"

"And he was killed by a vampire?" Aunt Candace continued, shamelessly ignoring my attempts to indicate to her to show a little more tact. "Yes, it is rather horrible. I wonder what he did to provoke them?"

The sound of a barstool scraping the floor broke through the uncomfortable silence that followed her words. The witch who'd been with Patti at the library got to her feet and began to walk towards the door.

"Aunt Candace," I hissed at her. To the others, I added, "I'm sorry. My aunt can be… tactless."

"She's still sensitive after what happened to Patti," said Rhonda. "She's having a tough time."

This might be my only chance to talk to her, so I pushed aside my discomfort and rose to my feet to follow the witch out of the pub.

"Hello," I said awkwardly. "I'm sorry about my aunt."

Corrine looked at me, her eyes brimming with tears. "Do I know you?"

"Yes. Well, no, but you were at the library the other day."

"Right. Patti and I…" She choked on the words.

"I'm sorry," I said awkwardly. "I didn't know her, but I'm sorry for your loss. I just wanted to ask you a question. She said you heard a rumour about—about the library at the pub, right? Was that here?"

"Why?" She sniffed, tears leaking from her eyes. "Yes, it must have been here that Patti heard it, but it hardly matters now, does it?"

"Can you tell me more?" I pressed. "I work at the library, and… and that corridor is dangerous, as you saw for yourself. I'd really like to know who started the rumour."

She didn't give off guilty vibes, exactly, and certainly wasn't a vampire either, but whoever had started the rumour had done so long before anyone had been killed. This must all be connected somehow.

"I don't know where it started," she said, but she didn't meet my eyes. "You know what rumours are like."

She's lying. I looked for Laney and saw her lurking near the door then hastily returned my attention to Corrine before she realised she was being watched. "And—did you know Olli?"

She flinched. "No, but it's horrible. What happened to him, I mean."

"It is." I had an inkling I wouldn't get anything more from her tonight, so I dropped the conversation and returned to the pub.

Inside, Aunt Candace had waylaid Shaw the barman and engaged him in conversation, so I made my way over to them.

Shaw greeted me with a grunt. "I was just telling your aunt that I haven't seen Olli since last night."

"He didn't come here today?" Then why had there been a smell of cocktails at the murder scene?

"Not yet, no." He polished a glass half-heartedly. "This is bad for business. My dad's not gonna be happy."

The enigmatic Shaw Senior hadn't made an appearance yet that I'd seen. "No. Olli was killed by a vampire, did you know?"

"I imagine they don't frequent this place," Aunt Candace said. "They prefer their cocktails mixed with blood."

He nearly dropped the glass. "Right."

I took my aunt's arm. "Come on. We should go."

"Karaoke starts soon."

"I never said I was staying for karaoke night," I said. "I was supposed to be out on a date with Xavier, actually."

Also, it was dinnertime, and I was starving, and it was clear that this place didn't serve anything that wasn't contained in a cocktail glass.

"How do you think I feel?" she huffed. "Maybe I shall go and see if Jaxon has changed his mind."

"Please don't." I turned to follow her out of the pub, where we found Laney waiting outside.

"That witch you were talking to," she said. "Corrine? She was lying to you when she said she didn't know where her friend heard the rumour."

"I thought so," I said. "What else did you read from her mind?"

"I don't know." She shook her head. "To tell you the truth, it kind of felt like she had some training to resist vampire mind reading. At least, her thoughts were clouded. Some of it might have been because she was drunk, though."

Suspicion arose. "Who would have taught her to hide her thoughts?"

More to the point, why would she have needed to?

"I don't know." Her forehead crinkled. "The way her thoughts were muddled, I could have sworn I saw something blocking me, and it wasn't like it usually is when someone tries to block me out. I saw this weird shadow in her head when I tried to go deeper into her thoughts."

"Shadow?" That rang a bell. "Wait. Did the guardian alter her memories?"

That might explain her confusion without any vampire-resisting training being involved, though it still left open the question of who'd started the rumour in the first place.

"I can go back in there and see if I can pick up on anything else, but it sounds like karaoke night is starting."

Sure enough, the crackle of a microphone sounded in the background, along with raised voices.

"No, we should go back to—Aunt Candace!" My aunt had turned away and began walking uphill. "Don't go back there. You know it won't do any good."

"I beg to differ," she said. "I need to tell Jaxon that Evangeline is manipulating him."

"I seriously doubt that's what's going on." Admittedly, being under Evangeline's watch might be the only way for him to avoid arrest for murder, but it wouldn't stop the rest of us having to deal with the consequences if Edwin wanted to question him again.

"Jaxon!" she suddenly yelled. "Why did my own character betray me?"

I shushed her. "You're always talking about your characters not doing what you tell them to. This is just a real-life extension of that."

"Don't be smart with me, Aurora."

"You wrote him that way, right?" I picked up speed as she continued uphill, and Laney caught up to me with ease.

"I'll keep an eye on her," Laney offered. "You should go and let your family know what's going on. They'll be worried."

"Yeah." They would. I'd been gone much longer than I'd planned, and I'd be returning with more confusion than answers, but it couldn't be helped. "Let me know if you find out anything else."

Namely, what Evangeline was playing at by keeping Jaxon in her home, whether as a guest or a prisoner.

When I walked into the library, the others were still gathered in the lobby.

"There you are," said Cass. "My mother was about to go to the jail to get you out."

"We didn't set foot near the jail," I told her. "Olli was killed by a vampire. Jaxon is currently hiding out in Evangeline's home."

"He's in Evangeline's home?" Aunt Adelaide asked. "I thought she cast him out."

"So did I." I shook my head. "I don't get it, but she seems to think he's better off under close watch. She wants to study him."

"That's not good news." She grimaced. "We can't have her learning about where he came from, nor the magic that powers the fourth-floor corridor."

"Speaking of which, we didn't have much luck finding the source of that rumour either." I recounted my encounter with Corrine. "Laney read her mind and said her thoughts were clouded. Might the guardian have messed with her memories?"

"It wouldn't be the first time." Cass lifted her gaze to the stairs and the upper floor. "If you ask me, we're better off without the vampire here."

"Except it's possible he killed two people," I said. "And the second *was* a vampire death."

"Who was the second victim again?" asked Estelle.

"A wizard called Olli," I said. "Another regular at the pub. If it wasn't Jaxon who killed him, it probably means there's a rogue vampire in town, so Evangeline is going to stay involved by default."

"Well, if Jaxon did it, Evangeline can lock him in the

dungeon with that Carlos Verdant," said Cass. "Problem solved."

"No way," I said. "We don't need the Founders finding out about him. If word gets out to the rest of them that we conjured up a vampire from a book, I can only imagine what they'll do with that information."

"Exactly," said Aunt Adelaide. "Is my sister at the vampires' home now?"

"Yeah." I grimaced. "It was that or let her hang out at karaoke night again. Laney is watching her."

"Why did you end up in the pub in the first place?" asked Cass.

"We went to check because the smell of those cocktails was all over the crime scene," I explained. "But the bartender said Olli hadn't been in there since last night."

"Those cocktails are potent," Estelle remarked. "I can still smell them on your clothes, Rory."

And to think I missed out on date night for this. While the possibility of Jaxon being arrested for murder remained less likely than before, how could we possibly get rid of him while he was under Evangeline's watchful eye?

10

Aunt Candace didn't show up for dinner and didn't return for the rest of the evening. Estelle and I threw ideas back and forth, most of which involved visiting the fourth floor and wishing for a miracle, but when we did go upstairs to the fourth floor, neither of us could come up with a wish that encompassed everything we needed.

"Where's the guardian?" Estelle paced along the corridor, but no signs of the shadowy figure appeared. "Has anyone seen her recently at all?"

"I guess she's been busy messing with the memories of people who started the rumours," I said. "But why not show herself to us? Even Aunt Candace?"

"I don't know." She bit her lower lip. "I also don't know if the guardian played a part in granting Aunt Candace's wish."

"If she did, she's bound to be having some regrets," I remarked. "Come to think of it, Aunt Candace mentioned it was far from the first time she'd tried to conjure up a fictional character. Why did this one work and not the others?"

The room only granted miracles, not answers, and since the latter was Sylvester's domain, it didn't fall under his realm of knowledge.

"I don't know, but I think your idea about conjuring up a cure for his spell over Aunt Candace might be our best option," she said. "Faster than brewing a potion too."

"Yeah, that's true. Though if Evangeline's under his spell as well, we'll have a much harder time convincing *her* to drink it."

"Let's hope it doesn't come to that, then." She stood back to let me write my wish on the door.

I pressed the point of the pen to the wooden surface and wrote, *I wish for a cure for Jaxon's spell over Aunt Candace.*

The words rippled and vanished into the wood. I waited for the door to open, but it didn't, and nothing in the corridor changed.

"Did I not get the words right?" I wondered. "Should I have been less specific? Or more?"

"I'll try asking for a potion." Estelle lifted her own pen and wrote on the door. *I'll wish for a potion that can remove mind control.*

The words rippled and vanished again, and this time the door swung inward. I peered over Estelle's shoulder and saw a table inside the small room, upon which sat a bottle scarcely bigger than my fist.

Estelle walked in and picked up the bottle. "I think this must be it."

"Why'd it work for you and not me?" Every time I assumed I knew how the corridor functioned, it confounded me again. "Never mind. Now all we need to do is figure out a way to get it to Aunt Candace."

We returned to the living quarters, and after Aunt Adelaide came up with a plan to get the potion to Aunt Candace by putting it in her coffee, I got out my dad's journal and tried to remember where I'd left off the last time. I'd found very little in there on the subject of the once-missing corridor, and the translation process was messy enough that I had to keep backtracking and rereading. Dad had skipped around a lot and gone back and annotated his old journal entries with digressions from his future self, and as a result, it was difficult to read the whole thing in chronological order.

I settled on the living room sofa and found the spot in the journal where I'd left off, in the middle of one of Dad's anecdotes. Generally, his journal entries recounted trips he'd taken to find rare books and return them to the library, and despite the vampires' ongoing fascination with the journal, most of the books Dad sought out on his adventures weren't the sort that would interest either Evangeline *or* the Founders. For instance, the book he'd been looking for in the journal entry where I'd left off had been enchanted so that you had to read it backwards to grasp the meaning and had been hidden in a small town in the Scottish Highlands.

Estelle came into the living room with two mugs of hot chocolate. "Hey, Rory. Found anything?"

"Nah, but a book that has to be read backwards is a new one."

"That's what he was looking for?" she asked.

"I know it's not completely relevant to what's going on now," I said, "but the corridor was still an unknown when he wrote this."

If nothing else, the journal was a temporary distraction from my worries about Aunt Candace and the vampires. I continued to work through the page of Dad's misadventures detailing when his train had broken down in the middle of the Scottish Highlands and wondered if he'd originally intended for me to read every word of his meanderings.

At the end of the page, I stopped at an annotation he'd

added later. *It reminds me of the case in York two years later of the book that had to be read sideways. Of course, that one had the added complication of birds flying out of the pages.*

"Huh?" Had I read that right? "Birds flying out of the pages?"

"Literally out of the pages?" Estelle asked. "Really?"

"Not sure." The annotation was dated, so I could skip ahead until I reached the right section and extracted the translated document. Most of the text concerned him getting lost on the way to York.

"How many times can one person's train break down?" I remarked. "He had worse luck than I did."

I skimmed down the page and halted. The train, it seemed, had broken down due to a swarm of giant birds that had shown up on the tracks.

It was easy to find the book, I read. *After all, the birds came* out *of the book itself.*

Wait. If the birds had come out of the book, had it been under a similar kind of spell to the one that had brought Aunt Candace's character to life? Like a Manifestation Curse?

Curiosity stirring, I read on. Then I extracted the page carefully and showed my cousin. "Estelle, what does this sound like to you?"

Her gaze panned over the page, and her eyes widened. "Birds flying out of a book? Is that the same as the spell we're dealing with now? Because it doesn't sound like the book your dad found originally came from the library."

"Exactly." I hadn't thought it was possible, but it made sense that the library wouldn't be the only place capable of that kind of magic. My family might be unusual, but for the first time, I found myself wondering if anyone else had the same kind of talent.

A thump sounded from outside the living quarters. Estelle lifted her head. "Someone's back."

"Aunt Candace?" I got up, tucked the journal under my arm, and tiptoed into the lobby, skirting around the large tree. It wasn't Aunt Candace but Laney, and she lay sprawled next to the trapdoor to the vampire's basement.

"Ow." She rose to her feet, scowling. "I swear that thing wasn't there when I walked in."

"It does that." I peered at the Christmas tree and spied Sylvester's owl eyes staring out of the branches. "Is Aunt Candace still hanging around the vampires' place?"

"Yeah," she said. "Sorry. Evangeline told me to go away, and I didn't want to push my luck."

"She told you to leave but let Aunt Candace stick around?"

"She wouldn't let either of us into the vampires' home," she said. "Honestly, it was kind of weird. I did see Jaxon inside, but he refused to come outside and speak to your aunt, and she's pretty crushed."

"Typical," I said. "Estelle and I conjured up a potion to remove the spell Jaxon cast on her, but we can't get it to her while she's outside the library."

"How—oh, you used the fourth-floor corridor?" She hesitated. "Speaking of which, I read your aunt's mind and... saw something weird."

"Weird how?"

She took in a breath. "The first night she went to the pub, she saw something outside that looked awfully like that creepy guardian from the corridor."

My heart missed a beat. "You thought you saw the guardian in Corrine's thoughts too."

"Yeah, and I thought I was mistaken, but this time was much clearer," she said. "It was outside the pub."

"That was *before* the first murder?" But after Patti and Corrine had shown up at the library looking for the corridor.

"Yeah," she said. "It was outside the pub. I couldn't tell how your aunt felt because her feelings were all muddled, thanks to that spell she's under."

"I bet," I murmured. "I hope she's careful out there."

If the guardian had been at the pub, had she lured Aunt Candace and Jaxon in there? Or had Jaxon already known? He had his origins in the same place as the guardian, but if the pair of them were working together, it opened up a new realm of unsettling possibilities.

How far was Grandma's guardian willing to go to protect the library's secrets?

———

That night, my dreams were full of strange manifestations coming out of books and flying around my head and shadowy figures in the dark that were neither Reapers nor vampires. I'd stayed up late translating the rest of the section of the journal I'd been working on and unintentionally over-slept, and I woke up to an apologetic message from Xavier about the previous night and letting me know he was free tonight for us to go on a date.

That cheered me up somewhat, and when I went down-stairs, I found Estelle at the breakfast table, a small bottle sitting next to the coffee pot.

"What were you going to do, spike Aunt Candace's coffee?" I asked.

"If she ever comes home."

"She didn't come back last night?" *Oh no.* "Don't tell me she camped out at the vampires' place."

"I hope not, but it's better than being locked in Evangeline's dungeon," she replied. "Did you finish that journal entry last night?"

"Yeah." I stacked toast on my plate, stifling a yawn. "Took a while, but I got to the end."

"How'd your dad manage to stop those birds from flying around?" she asked.

"He used a reversal spell," I answered. "He had to pick up a random notebook and pen to do it since he didn't have his wand or his Biblio-Witch Inventory with him."

"I'm surprised his magic worked that far from the library," she said. "I guess it can still function as long as there's a pen and paper within reach."

"Always good to know," I agreed. "Honestly, part of the reason I wanted to find out how it ended is because I thought the spell that created the birds might be similar to our magic. But that book didn't come from the library."

"No." Her brow furrowed. "Anyone can enchant a book, but biblio-witch magic is pretty specialized. Interesting that your dad was able to banish them."

"Yeah," I said. "I wondered if doing the same might work on Jaxon. But I know Sylvester told me that it has to be Aunt Candace who gets rid of him."

"You didn't ask directly about using biblio-witch magic, though, did you?"

"That's true."

After breakfast, I went searching for the Book of Questions. Sylvester's tree was quiet that morning, and when I opened the book and tumbled headfirst into its pages, silence greeted me on the other side.

"I have a question," I went on, undeterred by the lack of any response. "Is it possible for one of us to use biblio-witch magic to banish a creation who came out of a book without needing to be near the spell that created them?"

"You already know the answer to that," said the owl's voice. "Really, you need to try harder with your questions."

"That means yes." My heart lifted marginally. "Is there a catch? Can we just use a banishment spell and send Jaxon packing?"

"You can try," he said, "but I rather think the effectiveness will depend upon whether the person who summoned him takes objection to you trying to banish their creation."

"Oh." Some of my optimism faded. Nobody had wanted a swarm of birds all over the train tracks, and whoever had actually been responsible for conjuring them out of the book's pages hadn't been present. At least, Dad hadn't mentioned them. With Aunt Candace strenuously opposing anyone who tried to get rid of her vampire companion, would a banishment spell have the same effect, even when cast by another biblio-witch?

The room tipped over, and I fell back out, landing sprawled beside the front desk.

Estelle peered down at me. "Any luck?"

"Apparently, it's true." I rose to my feet. "We can get rid of him by writing a banishment word or tapping it in our Biblio-Witch Inventory, but Sylvester implied that Aunt Candace might try to fight back."

"Still," she said. "We can keep that plan in reserve in case the potion doesn't work. We need to find Aunt Candace first."

"Yeah, we should go and find her." I fervently hoped Evangeline hadn't lost her temper outright and locked Aunt Candace in the dungeon, but both of them were behaving unpredictably at best lately. "Where's your mum? She'll have to open the library while we're gone."

"She went upstairs to deal with a problem on the second floor." She glanced at the clock. "It's almost opening time."

"I guess it's too much to ask of the universe that we don't get any visitors as soon as the doors open."

The answer was *yes*, apparently. No sooner had the clock struck nine than a group of students came sailing in. Estelle hastened to help them find the textbooks they needed while I called Jet and asked him to fly to the vampires' place to look for Aunt Candace until I could go and join him.

At the tail end of a group of students came a witch wearing a hooded cloak, which she removed when she was inside, revealing a streak of bright pink in her hair. A jolt of recognition hit me. *Corrine.* She approached me, a decidedly shifty expression on her face.

"Erm, hi," I said. "Can I help you?"

"I wanted to talk to you," she mumbled. "Last night, I was upset."

"I understand why." Questions crowded my mind, multiplying when she cast a glance around the lobby as though afraid someone was listening in. "Is there something you wanted to ask me?"

"Is your aunt in? The one from the pub?"

"No, not at the moment." I decided not to say *where* she was.

"She's with her visitor?" she guessed. "Jaxon?"

"I don't know," I evaded. "Any reason?"

"I was just wondering," she mumbled. "I wanted to... to talk to you alone."

"What about?" I asked. "About Patti? Or Olli?"

"Kind of." Her mouth turned down at the corners. "Olli was killed by a vampire, I heard."

"That's what they said," I said carefully. "What is it?"

"That Jaxon." She took in a breath. "He seems... odd. Where did you say he came from?"

"He's visiting my aunt. You'll have to ask her." My skin prickled. "He's not here either, if you wanted to talk to him."

"I don't," she said. "I… The night Patti was killed, I saw him talking to Olli. Olli was asking him questions about being a vampire."

My mouth went dry. "He was?"

"Yeah," she said. "I forgot. Honestly, my memories of that night are pretty foggy, but it was definitely him."

"Olli wanted to become a vampire?" And he'd chosen to ask Jaxon. Had he figured out that Jaxon wasn't a typical vampire?

Just then, the library doors flew wide open, and Aunt Candace came in, beaming, with Jaxon at her side.

11

Aunt Candace eyed Corrine. "Oh, it's you."

Corrine gasped and then ran straight out of the library without looking back. Aunt Candace laughed while I peered at the vampire, confused. "I thought he couldn't come outside in daylight without catching on fire."

"Oh, I draped my cloak over his head," said Aunt Candace. She looked tired, but her bright expression banished any hope I might have had that she'd let Jaxon leave willingly. "He's fine."

The vampire looked dead on his feet—pun intended—and was practically falling asleep on Aunt Candace's shoulder. After what Corrine had just told me, I hadn't been prepared to face him again nor had I had a moment to consider how to broach the question of his last conversation with Olli before the wizard's murder.

"Oh, Aunt Candace." Estelle ran into the lobby, arms full of books she'd been retrieving for the visiting students. "We were going to go looking for you. Have you been out all night?"

"I thought you were with the vampires." Specifically, with Evangeline. Hadn't she wanted to keep Jaxon under her watchful eye, whether she thought him responsible for the murders or not? What had changed her mind?

"Oh, it was just a misunderstanding," Aunt Candace said. "I think I shall go to bed."

"Wait." I scrambled to pull my thoughts together. "Corrine was just here. She said that Olli—you know, the wizard who died—was talking to Jaxon at the pub the other night and asking him questions about being a vampire. Is it true?"

"Who?" asked Jaxon blearily.

"Olli. The wizard who was wearing a top hat."

Aunt Candace gave me the evil eye. "Now, Rory, there's no need to ask difficult questions. We're both very tired."

"I know, but I wanted to ask before you go to sleep," I said. "Did Olli want to become a vampire?"

Jaxon's voice was somewhat slurred. "Yes, he wanted to know the details of the transformation process."

"That's enough," Aunt Candace said sharply, taking his arm. "Ignore her, Jaxon."

She half carried him to the living quarters, and they both vanished upstairs.

"I thought Evangeline wanted him where she could keep an eye on him," Estelle said. "What made her change her mind?"

"I was wondering that. And why he changed *his* mind." I'd thought he'd forsaken the library altogether. "Do you have that potion? We need to give it to Aunt Candace while she's here."

"In the kitchen." She ran to the living quarters, and I followed, hoping that Aunt Candace wouldn't suspect anything. We needed to undo that spell on her before Jaxon was able to kill again.

Of course, I was still assuming he *was* the killer, but what of Evangeline? Hadn't she suspected him too? I definitely needed to pay her a visit, and she'd certainly want to know Olli had been asking questions about how to become a vampire. Like Laney, though, she wouldn't be awake during the day.

Estelle ran upstairs with the coffee pot and returned within a minute, shaking her head. "I don't think she's going to drink that until she wakes up. She really was out all night."

"And Evangeline let her?" I asked. "Doesn't sound like her, but neither does letting Jaxon go."

"No. Did he… Might he have used his mind control on her?"

"She told me it didn't affect her." What game was she playing? "I'd go and see her now, but she won't thank me for waking her up."

"No," she said. "Better to wait until later."

"I'll have to tell her Olli was asking questions about becoming a vampire too," I said. "I don't get the impression she's been focused on investigating his death, despite Edwin leaving the questioning to her."

"I guess it's tricky when the person who dies isn't a vampire and the perpetrator probably isn't one of her people," she said.

Probably. My skin prickled. Was the killer right here in the library? If the potion didn't work, we needed another way to get rid of him, and while my dad's journal had given me the idea of using a banishment spell, I hadn't yet learned to use biblio-witch magic for that purpose. And a few birds were likely easy to get rid of compared to banishing a person, even a fictional one.

He's asleep, I reminded myself. *He's not a threat to anyone at the moment.*

Not yet anyway.

"One of us should let Cass know they're back," said Estelle. "I know she was worried about Aunt Candace."

"Really?" I raised a brow. "I didn't think she even noticed."

"Oh, she noticed," said Estelle. "I saw her briefly in the middle of the night when I came downstairs to see if Aunt Candace had come back in. I'm almost certain she paid the fourth floor a visit last night."

"Hope it didn't backfire on her." Though I had a hard time thinking of anything worse than what Aunt Candace had done. "I'll tell her."

I went upstairs to the third floor and the Magical Creatures Division.

My cousin answered after the first knock on the door. "I know Aunt Candace is back. I heard her nauseatingly cheerful voice from up here."

"Then you know she brought Jaxon with her. They're both asleep, but..." I gestured at the fourth-floor corridor entrance, which was pale purple today. "Have you been up there recently?"

"Yes, but I didn't make any wishes. Sylvester warned me off."

"He did that to me too." Though he hadn't yesterday, come to think of it. "I wonder why."

"He usually has good reason."

"Yes." A sudden suspicion seized me. "I had an idea, but you'll probably think I'm unhinged."

"What is it?"

"Laney read Aunt Candace's mind yesterday..." I paused when her eye twitched. I knew the mind reading was a sore issue with Cass, who liked her privacy and had obtained an anti-mind-reading pendant for that very purpose. I ploughed ahead. "She saw the guardian outside the Cocktail Cauldron on the night Patti was killed. Apparently, it was waiting outside when Aunt Candace and Jaxon first got there. I wondered if it might have lured them there."

She blinked. "The guardian lured them into the pub? Why?"

"Possibly because it's the place where Patti and Corrine heard the rumour," I said. "You know, about the corridor. If the guardian has been roaming around messing with people's memories…"

"Then we don't have to worry about them spreading rumours any longer, do we?"

"We don't know where the rumour started," I reminded her. "Also, Corrine was here earlier, and she told me that the last murder victim from yesterday was asking Jaxon questions about the process of becoming a vampire."

Cass swore. "And Evangeline still let him go?"

"I don't know if she knows. She can't read his mind, but I get the impression she has her own agenda." Not that that was anything new. "Estelle was going to give Aunt Candace the potion, but she's asleep. Otherwise, I wondered if we could try getting rid of Jaxon ourselves using biblio-witch magic. My dad did the same years ago when he found a bunch of birds someone had brought out of a book. I read it in the journal last night."

"I already tried that," she said. "The same as I tried writing a wish on that door to get rid of him. Didn't work."

"What? You did?" I stared at her. "When was this?"

"A couple of days ago. It doesn't matter, does it? I already figured it wouldn't work."

"And then you tried a banishment spell?"

"Of course I did," she said in impatient tones. "You might not have reached that level, but a banishment spell was one of the first things to come to mind. Evidently Aunt Candace's will to keep Jaxson alive is stronger than our desire to be rid of him."

"Ouch." That had to sting, enough for me to overlook her implied insult. "What if all of us except Aunt Candace used a banishment spell at the same time?"

"All of us against Aunt Candace?" She shook her head. "I wouldn't count on it."

Damn. That meant the vampire would stick around as long as Aunt Candace wanted him to. Now that they'd made up, who knew how long that would be? "Do you have any other ideas?"

"Yes, arrest the vampire while he's sleeping. *Why* did Evangeline let him go?"

"I wish I knew." She must have a plan, but knowing Evangeline, she wouldn't elect to let the rest of us in on it, not even Laney. "I can't talk to any of the vampires until they wake up, and Corrine took off as soon as Aunt Candace came back. I'm not sure if she might have more to tell me."

"Will she be at the pub?"

"During the day? I doubt it." Even the karaoke club wasn't that hardcore, though Shaw the bartender never seemed to leave the place.

"I bet she'll keep nightly hours if she's an aspiring vampire too."

"I'm not sure she is." But Jaxon had come back while she'd been here. Had his vampire super sense enabled him to hear anything she'd told me? "I think it's worth me learning a banishment spell."

"Sure, but if you try to banish a whole *person* on your first attempt, you'll end up sending half the library into an alternative dimension or something."

"Is that even possible?" I asked, but she had a point, admittedly. "Right. I'll ask your mum."

"You do that." She retreated into the Magical Creatures Division, the door closing behind her.

My attention slid over to the entrance to the fourth-floor

corridor, my heart stuttering in my chest as questions spun around my mind, unanswered. Was the guardian up there right now, or was she out roaming around Ivory Beach? Unlike the vampires, she didn't need to sleep.

Wishing we had a way to directly communicate with her, I climbed downstairs to the lobby. Sylvester had finally come out of the tree and perched behind the desk in his usual spot. "There's not much holiday cheer around here, is there?" he asked.

"Did you expect there to be?" I picked up the Book of Questions and put it back on its shelf, already wondering if I should have chosen a different question for that day. "Among other things, we probably have a murderer sleeping upstairs."

"Obviously. She's been here for months."

"You know I didn't mean Laney." I also didn't like thinking of how she'd staked several vampires in defence of my life. For an instant, I imagined her doing the same to Jaxon and immediately felt sickened at the very idea. It might be possible to banish him in the touch of a single word, but that didn't make him less of a living and breathing person. Killer or not. "Where's Aunt Adelaide?"

"I believe she's helping your cousin devise a way to poison Candace."

"Poison?" My heart lurched. "The potion isn't poison. Why would you say that?"

"I wouldn't trust anything that came out of that place," he said.

Was he being serious? "The guardian wouldn't harm any of us." Would she?

He hooted with laughter. "Your *face*, Rory."

"You *were* joking." I swatted at him and got clawed across my palm for my trouble. "Sylvester, now is not the time."

Did he share any of my suspicions? Namely, that the guardian *had* been involved in two deaths? If not directly then through luring Jaxon to the source of the rumours. And being involved in creating him in the first place. A shiver ran down my spine.

"You have no sense of humour," he said.

"Two people are already dead, and the killer might be here in the library," I pointed out. "Also, you didn't mention that it would take more than one of us to banish Jaxon using biblio-witch magic."

"To do what?" Aunt Adelaide walked downstairs, a harried expression on her face. "Sorry, did you say biblio-witch magic?"

"Last night, I was translating my dad's journal, and I found a passage where he had to get rid of a bunch of birds that came out of the pages of a book," I explained. "He was able to banish them with biblio-witch magic even though he wasn't the person who brought them to life."

"He was?" Her eyes widened a fraction. "He didn't have his Biblio-Witch Inventory?"

"He used an ordinary pen and paper," I said. "I asked Sylvester if we could do the same to Jaxon, but Cass told me that it would probably take more than one of us to pull it off and we'd be up against Aunt Candace's belief in her own character."

She sucked in a breath. "Yes, that's what I thought. It's why I didn't suggest it earlier."

"I also haven't learned that spell yet," I added. "As Cass pointed out to me."

"I can teach you," Estelle offered. "Banishment has a lot of potential to go wrong, though."

"Cass told me the same," I said. "Do you think it would work, though? I know a person is probably harder to banish than those birds Dad had to get rid of."

Sylvester made a snorting noise. "Yes, a little."

I ignored him. "Also, Cass said it's essentially a battle of wills between us and Aunt Candace, which we're bound to lose."

"She might be right." Aunt Adelaide's expression was unreadable. Had *she* encountered any spells similar to the one that my dad had found? "That spell is advanced, but I think you're ready for it."

As it turned out, banishment spells were complicated enough that it took half the afternoon for Estelle to teach me how to use one. By the end of our lesson, which was punctuated by detours to fetch books and return them to their rightful places, I'd successfully used the spell on a lot of bits of paper that wouldn't be missed, but I hadn't quite dared progress to anything larger.

"You've made good progress," Estelle reassured me. "It's better to be cautious than to accidentally banish a book that we need."

"Or half the library."

"Oh, that won't happen. Did Cass say that, by any chance?"

"She did." I should have figured she'd been exaggerating. "Do you know if Aunt Candace is awake yet?"

"I haven't heard anything, but I left the coffee pot in her room."

"Good." My heart gave a jolt as Sylvester's earlier comment echoed in my mind. "I think. What if the potion doesn't have the effect we need? The fourth-floor room... it's not been the most reliable lately."

"If it gave us the potion, it should work," she said. "Like when you cured Laney."

Right. I shook off the unease. The room—and the guardian—wouldn't harm any of us, including Aunt Candace.

As we were closing the library for the day, Aunt Candace came downstairs with Jaxon close behind her. The vampire was wide awake and alert, and the pair made straight for the door.

"Where are you going this time?" Had she drunk any of the coffee? I couldn't tell, but her proximity to Jaxon indicated that she was no less attached to him than she'd been earlier.

"Where else?" she asked. "I want to make it quite clear to Evangeline that she's not to harass Jaxon any further."

"You what?" Had the coffee had no effect, or hadn't she drunk it at all? "You can't threaten Evangeline. What even happened between you three?"

"That," said Aunt Candace, "is no concern of yours."

"It is. Evangeline is the vampires' leader, and she's supposed to be investigating Olli's murder." I glanced at Jaxon, but his face was impassive. "He was killed by a vampire, and he wanted to become one himself."

"Who wouldn't?" Aunt Candace's smile was back. "Fine, we'll stay away from Evangeline. We still have plenty of places to explore. Shall we visit the beach, Jaxon?"

Are you sure he won't run off this time?

I didn't say so aloud, but her narrowed eyes told me that she'd guessed what I was thinking. And it couldn't be more obvious that she was as besotted with him as ever.

As the pair of them vanished outside, Laney emerged from the living quarters. "Hey, Rory. Was that your aunt?"

"Yeah, you slept through her coming back."

"With Jaxon?" She blinked a couple times, as though waking up from sleep. "Wait. Evangeline let him go?"

"They wouldn't tell me the details, but apparently, she did."

"That's bizarre." Her brow furrowed. "Did he cast a spell over her like he did on Aunt Candace?"

"I thought the same, but…" I paused as my cousin ducked

out from behind the shelf near the desk. "Estelle, Aunt Candace and Jaxon just went out."

"What?" she said. "Aunt Candace, she drank the coffee. I saw her."

"Did it have no effect?" I swivelled to Laney. "Estelle gave her the potion that was supposed to erase the effects of the spell."

"Might it take a bit of time to work?" asked Laney. "Some potions do, right?"

"They do," said Estelle. "Since I got the potion from the fourth floor, it didn't say."

"Then it might still work." We couldn't count on it, though. "I need to speak to Evangeline anyway. It turns out that Olli was asking Jaxon questions about what it was like to turn into a vampire the first night they went to the pub."

"Whoa." Laney's eyes widened. "Olli wanted to turn into a vampire?"

"Yeah, according to Corrine. She came to the library earlier," I explained. "Then Aunt Candace and Jaxon showed up, and she ran off."

"I bet," said Laney. "Olli wanted to become a vampire. Might Patti have wanted the same?"

"I don't know, and I'm not sure about Corrine either."

"I didn't see anything about wanting to be a vampire when I read her mind," Laney said, "but like I said, her thoughts were pretty clouded. I can try again or just ask outright. I mean, if they want to know what it's like being a vamp, I'm the obvious person to ask."

"That's true," I said, "but we'll talk to Evangeline first."

I had a long list of questions, but at the top of the list was why she'd let Jaxon go.

Laney inclined her head. "Anyone who wants to turn into a vampire is a major red flag."

I didn't need to be able to read her mind to know she was

thinking of her own induction into the magical world via one of the Founders' parties, where countless normals mingled and hoped to join the ranks of the living dead.

While it was possible that Olli had been interested in turning into a vampire for his own reasons, there was no way to be certain that he'd come up with the idea on his own. And why had he decided to ask Jaxon questions and not one of the locals? Because he'd suspected something was off about the vampire or because he'd been too scared to get near Evangeline's house? I would never be able to ask Olli himself, but suspicions lurked in the back of my mind as Laney and I left the library.

My family gave me the usual warnings to be careful while I messaged Xavier, letting him know where I was going in case we ended up coming back later than planned. Our date wasn't set for another hour, but guilt nagged at me when I walked past the gate to the cemetery.

The Cocktail Cauldron was already packed out, and I stopped to peer through the grimy window. "What're they doing, celebrating Olli's life the same way they did with Patti?"

"They'll really take any excuse for a party," Laney said. "Want to check in there first?"

"No, we'll talk to…" I trailed off when I followed her gaze up the high street and saw Evangeline herself approaching the pub at a purposeful stride.

12

"Aurora." Evangeline gave me a brief nod as she walked into the pub, and I heard a chorus of gasps from inside. No surprise. The head vampire didn't even need to speak to terrify the living daylights out of everyone.

Heart swooping, I slipped into the pub behind her, with Laney at my side.

"No need to stop on my account." Her gaze swept over the room, and then she spoke. "I won't be here for long, but I heard that someone among your number was asking questions about being turned into a vampire. Is that correct?"

There was a collective intake of breath, but nobody said a word as she surveyed the room with deceptive calmness. Nor did anyone move. Her words held us all captive, frozen to the spot.

"That same individual later died," Evangeline added after a prolonged pause. "An unfortunate accident, no doubt, but I would like to make it clear that it was not one of my fellow vampires who was responsible for his death."

A visible ripple of unease went through the crowd, but still, nobody spoke.

"In fact," she went on, "there is the chance that the unfortunate death was not the result of a vampire attack at all. The bite wounds on his neck were not the cause of his demise."

What? Did she really think Olli's death hadn't been the result of a vampire attack? I scanned the room and spied Jaxon standing with Aunt Candace behind a group of other karaoke goers, but I couldn't read his expression from here.

"In the meantime," said Evangeline, "I'll invite anyone who might be curious about the details of becoming one of my fellow vampires to ask me directly. We are quite willing to answer questions."

She gave the room another sweeping gaze and left a shocked silence in her wake as she turned to leave. I unfroze and caught the door before it closed behind her. Laney, too, followed the vampires' leader outside.

"What was that about?" she asked, echoing my thoughts. "Do you really want everyone from the pub showing up at your house asking questions about becoming a vampire? Or were you trying to scare them off?"

"And do you really think Olli wasn't killed by a vampire?" I moved after Evangeline as she strode away from the pub. Laney kept pace with her, but my human legs hadn't a hope of matching her speed. "Wait! I needed to talk to you anyway."

"Here is hardly an appropriate place, is it?"

"No, but it's urgent." I followed her up the high street, my breath puffing out as I fought to keep up. "Aren't you in the least bit curious about what *did* kill Olli, if not one of your own vampires? Because if it isn't Jaxon either, then there's a rogue... Slow down!"

Evangeline ignored me. Gaining speed, she crested the top of the high street; Laney flashed me an apologetic look over her shoulder as she followed the head vampire around the corner. I kept walking, my legs protesting, until a scream rang out behind me.

I rotated on my heel. *That came from the pub.*

I ran downhill, gasping for breath, and skidded to a halt outside. With the vampire's departure, everyone had unfrozen and raised their voices to high volume, but a second scream cut through all other noise.

"She's dead!" The shout was echoed back and forth as I entered the pub, scanning for Aunt Candace and Jaxon. A growing crowd had gathered near the door to the beer garden at the back, and I made my way through, my heart hammering.

Through a gap in the crowd, I glimpsed a body sprawled on the ground outside. *Corrine.* She lay on her front, unmoving. *Where's Xavier?* If she was dead, where was the Reaper?

"He killed her!" shouted a witch who'd climbed onto one of the outside tables, pointing an accusing finger at Jaxon. He and Aunt Candace stood amid the crowd nearest to the body. My mouth went dry when several people turned in their direction.

"That's three people who've turned up dead since you started coming here," added the witch. "You found Patti too. Are you killing us off?"

"Did you kill Olli too?" someone else shouted.

Where *was* Xavier? As I watched, heart sinking, the crowd began to converge on the pair of them until Aunt Candace and Jaxon stood with their backs against the fence encasing the beer garden. Jaxon's fangs were out, and while the clamour of voices drowned out all other noise, I knew he was hissing at them. He didn't think he could take on that many people at once, did he?

"Stop!" I reached for my wand—for all the good that would do—and Jaxon *moved.* With a vampire's dizzying speed, he was through the back gate and out of the beer garden in the time it took to blink.

The onlooking karaoke club members stared at the fence, where he'd left Aunt Candace standing alone in the face of the seething crowd, and then someone shouted, "After him!"

Recovering, the crowd headed towards an open gate at the back of the beer garden. Aunt Candace watched them with a dazed expression on her face, and I pushed my way to her side.

"Wait. Don't go after him." I snagged her arm as she began to follow the crowd. "They're after you, too, remember?"

She's supposed to be cured. Why did the potion have no effect?

More to the point, where was Xavier? Corrine was dead, wasn't she? I didn't dare take my eyes off my aunt, but as the crowd continued to leave the beer garden, a few people lingered behind, including Rhonda. The troll knocked a couple of wizards aside as she shuffled over to Aunt Candace.

"Did you know?" she asked, her voice thick. "Did you know Jaxon killed Patti?"

"He didn't," Aunt Candace insisted.

"Yes, he did." A second voice spoke up from much closer to the ground as Trina, the elf, elbowed her way through the crowd. "Jaxon killed them."

"We'll make him pay for it," someone said.

"Good luck catching a vampire at full speed," Aunt Candace retorted. "He's long gone."

"We should call the police." I flashed my aunt a pleading look then turned to Rhonda. "We had nothing to do with what happened to your friend. I'm sorry."

"Three people are dead," said Rhonda. "Because of *your* friend."

"I'm sorry." I tugged on Aunt Candace's arm. "He put her under a spell. Please—"

A shadow fell over the beer garden. All eyes turned towards the pub's entrance as darkness spread outward, and Xavier stepped out, his scythe in his hands.

He's later than usual.

Out of the corner of my eye, I saw Aunt Candace duck through the gate and leave the beer garden. Cursing inwardly, I followed her. "Wait. Jaxon has already gone."

"He'll wait for me."

"He won't." *Why* hadn't the potion worked on her? "Come back to the library."

"I can't. Jaxon needs me."

And before I could react, Aunt Candace pulled out her Biblio-Witch Inventory, tapped a word—and vanished.

"Rory." Xavier ducked out of the beer garden behind me. "We'd better go."

Nothing for it. We ran down the alleyway and emerged onto the high street. The mob had already disappeared uphill, though I heard raised voices drifting over the rooftops.

"They've lost their minds," I gasped out. "Why'd you show up late? Did your boss keep you waiting at home?"

"No, but I need to tell him about this."

"Why? In case someone else dies?" My thoughts collided. "Did Corrine say anything to you? Wait. When did she die?"

"About a minute ago. Why?"

"But that means she wasn't dead when they originally found her body." My mind reeled as we walked downhill, pausing at the cemetery gate.

"I do need to tell my boss," he said apologetically. "You should be okay getting back to the library from here? Or should I walk you there?"

"No, I'll be fine," I said numbly, my thoughts ricocheting from the mob of angry karaoke goers to Jaxon and Aunt Candace and then to the vampires. If the mob had gone straight to Evangeline's house, I hoped Laney had managed to get out of their way. "I need to call the police. Or someone does."

"I will," he offered. "And I'll come to the library as soon as I'm done. I'm sorry."

"Don't be." Our ruined date night was nothing compared to everything else. "I'll see you in a bit."

I ran back to the library, hardly stopping to breathe. I'd half expected to hear the pounding of feet on my path, but they'd all gone in the opposite direction, up the high street. Were they going to Evangeline's home? She might have claimed disinterest and had even seemingly tolerated Aunt Candace's presence the previous night, but that didn't mean she would tolerate a mob arriving on her doorstep.

Estelle jumped when I burst into the library. "Rory, what happened?"

"Evangeline screwed everything up," I wheezed, clutching a stitch in my chest. "Corrine's dead, and everyone blamed Jaxon. He ran off, and so did Aunt Candace."

"Slow down, Rory." She beckoned me into the living quarters, where Aunt Adelaide joined us and I explained the whole fiasco.

Xavier still wasn't back by the time I was done, and I was starting to worry that the Grim Reaper had refused to let him come here after all.

"How did Corrine die?" asked Aunt Adelaide. "Do you know?"

I shook my head. "No. I'll have to ask Xavier, if his boss lets him leave. Laney's out there too. She went after Evangeline."

"Good." Cass stepped into view. "Someone has to."

"Except that might be where the mob went too," I said. "I don't know how much you heard—"

"All of it," she said. "I bet Evangeline can take on those

karaoke goers without breaking a sweat. They're idiots if they think they can outdo a vampire."

"Or two vampires. They went after Jaxon, remember?"

"And so did Aunt Candace."

"I know." Worry squirmed in my chest. "They're more likely to catch up to her than to him, and I doubt he'll come back to find her. He left her to face them alone."

"And she's still under his spell?" Estelle said. "I don't understand why the cure didn't work."

"Maybe she's beyond curing," said Cass. "And Jaxon is now a murderer three times over."

"Then why did Evangeline let him go?" I hoped Laney had managed to corner her for long enough to ask some questions, but letting Jaxon escape wasn't her only perplexing decision. "She also showed up at the pub and pretty much told everyone at karaoke that they're welcome to come to her house and ask questions about becoming a vampire. And she implied it wasn't a vampire who killed Olli at all, but I guess they decided Jaxon was guilty anyway."

"She's not infallible," said Estelle. "I bet Evangeline will go after Jaxon herself when she realises she was mistaken."

"Has anyone called the police?" asked Aunt Adelaide.

"I don't know," I said. "You'd think someone would have— Shaw, maybe. He's the bartender." And probably the only person left in the pub, at this rate.

"Then I'll go myself." She left the living quarters and made for the front door. "Can you make sure nobody comes into the library while I'm gone?"

"Of course," said Estelle. "But you're going alone?"

"Don't." I moved after her. "The karaoke goers... if they went after Aunt Candace, they might come for the rest of us too."

"They can certainly try," said Aunt Adelaide, and she opened the door and vanished into the night.

I gaped after her. "What's she thinking?"

"She'll have a plan," Estelle said. "Count on it."

I hoped she was right, because the library might become a potential target too. As little as I wanted that to happen, I had the sinking suspicion that since the library had caused this, maybe only the library could end it.

13

As minutes passed and Xavier still didn't return, I found my feet carrying me towards the stairs up to the fourth floor. Nobody stopped me, though I glimpsed Cass following me at a distance. When we reached the third floor, I turned to face her. "You don't need to tell me that you think I'm making a mistake by going back up there. I just don't see any other options."

"I wasn't planning to," she said. "What were you going to wish for?"

"A miracle," I replied. "I don't know, but we can't count on the vampires to get us out of this one, and it looks like the Grim Reaper is refusing to let Xavier leave too."

"I wouldn't count out the vampires," she said. "Laney will be back here as soon as she realises what's going on."

"Are you sure?" I asked, surprised at her implied faith in Laney. The pair had had a rocky relationship since my best friend's arrival in the library, to say the least. "Well, I'm not going to let our family get targeted by a mob if it turns out Evangeline is intentionally throwing us under the bus so that she can go after the enemy herself. Which is the only explanation that makes sense, at this point."

"I know she's a manipulator," said Cass. "I'm not going to claim otherwise."

"That doesn't mean she was right to let Jaxon go," I said. "And if he *is* the killer, she willingly let him hurt someone else."

"We already knew she has a skewed sense of morality," Cass said. "If you ask me, her public display was intended to scare the enemy out of hiding."

"Except it didn't work." Just like the cure hadn't. "I don't expect her to lift a finger to help us, but it'd be nice to think we had at least one all-powerful immortal entity on our side."

"Xavier's on our side. He'll escape his boss when he can get away from it."

"I know." I'd been thinking of the guardian as well as the vampires. *Was she helping us at all? Or did she intentionally leave Aunt Candace under Jaxon's spell?*

"Did someone mention all-powerful immortal entities?" Sylvester enquired, fluttering down to land on a nearby bookshelf.

"Yes." I'd already used up my question, but maybe he would take pity on me and lend a hand. I could dream. "I assume you heard what a mire of manticore dung we've landed in."

"I rather think it's mostly your aunt Candace who stands knee-deep in manticore dung."

"Keep my manticore out of it," said Cass. "He's right, though, Rory. This is on her."

"No, it's on that bloody corridor," I said. "And the guardian, too, for not stopping this. I don't know if it's her who's responsible for granting the wishes or something else, but it's not like I can ask."

I couldn't even ask the Book of Questions because its

knowledge didn't encompass this corridor. For whatever reason, Grandma hadn't wanted Sylvester to know.

The owl clucked his beak. "Did I not warn you against placing your faith in that deceitful place?"

"You didn't warn Estelle when she wished for the cure." I raised my arms in defence when he loomed threateningly over me. "I wasn't blaming you. I was just pointing out that you *did* warn me off making any wishes, and Cass too. Did you know the cure wouldn't work?"

"There's no need to sound so accusing." He sounded insulted. "I have no way of knowing whether anything from that room will be effective."

I was surprised he would admit to that much. "Then why'd you follow me up here?"

"To stop you from making a foolish decision out of a misguided attempt to fix someone else's mistake."

"What else am I supposed to do?" I asked. "Evangeline turned on us. The guardian is untrustworthy. And I don't need to hear 'I told you so.' Fictional or not, Jaxon committed murder, three times over. That makes it our family's responsibility to fix as much of the damage as possible."

He gave a sigh. "I'll let you get on with it, then."

He took flight in a flutter of tawny wings. Cass raised a brow at me. "Still want to make a wish?"

"No, but I do want to find the guardian."

Can I wish to find her?

If the guardian was avoiding us, that might be my last option to corner her. I crossed the third floor, my apprehension building. The door stood in shadow, its paint now jet-black. I reached for the handle, half expecting resistance, but it swung open soundlessly.

Heart in my throat, I climbed the stairs to the fourth-floor corridor and paced to the door I needed. I reached into my pocket, pulled out a pen, and pressed the point to the wooden surface.

I wish for the guardian to appear.

Movement fluttered in the corner of my eye. I jumped. The guardian hovered above the carpeted floor, as if she'd been there all along, and a shiver raced down my spine as a chill breeze swept through the air, like a threat or a warning.

"Have you been erasing people's memories?" The words rushed out of me. "Or worse? Have you been going to any lengths to cover up the library's secrets? Even… murder?"

The corridor picked up the faintest echo of my words, and the chill in the air intensified.

"I know you were erasing the memories of the people at the pub," I went on. "You led Jaxon there, too, didn't you? In fact, you're the one who helped my aunt summon him in the first place."

The breeze intensified, forcing me to take a step back, towards the stairs. Aunt Candace had been trying to summon one of her characters for months, yet the corridor had only granted her wish when it had another purpose. Protecting the library's secrets, no matter the cost.

I staggered back a few more steps. "I'm right, aren't I? You sabotaged our attempts to cure Aunt Candace because it was more useful for her to be under Jaxon's spell."

A gust of wind hit me head-on, and this time I went flying straight off my feet. I hit the wall, gasping, and my nerve fled. I turned and ran, a gust pursuing me until I tripped over the edge of the stairs, arms flailing.

As I began to fall, my body halted abruptly. I reeled back, catching my balance on the step.

"Whoa." Cass peered up at me, her Biblio-Witch Inventory in her hand. "That was close."

"Thanks." I hurried downstairs before another attack hit me, my heart racing. "Thanks. The guardian…"

"I did warn you." Sylvester waited outside, perched on a shelf outside the Magical Creatures Division.

I whirled on him. "Yes, you did, but you haven't been much help either. And don't tell me to use the Book of Questions. I can't do that until tomorrow, and I don't even want to think of what else might happen before then."

"Then don't."

I gave a despairing snort. "Sure, I just won't think about the impending disaster. Oh, and that we have a monster in the library that set a vampire loose to *murder* people for sharing the library's secrets with outsiders."

"Your propensity to jump to conclusions is astonishing," said the owl. "Do you truly think your grandmother would harm anyone?"

My mouth parted. "Well, no. Though I never met her. Also, the guardian isn't her, and neither is Jaxon. They're creations of the library."

"Technically, you're as much a creation of the library as they are," said the owl. "You've lived here for long enough, haven't you?"

"I'm not the one wanted for murder," I said. "And I didn't come out of a book."

"You are depressingly literal."

What *was* the owl talking about? Jaxon had been created by the library. And while I certainly hadn't, I supposed my magic had, in a way. Biblio-witch magic was at the root of the library and had formed the foundations of the spell that had led to its very creation. Maybe the same applied to the fourth-floor corridor, as both had the same source. Namely, my grandmother. But that didn't erase the damage they'd caused.

"Let me get this straight," said Cass. "You think the guardian killed all those people?"

"I don't know what to think," I admitted. "I don't want to

believe Grandma would have created something that would commit murder either, but who else killed those people?"

"Ask Sylvester."

"I already used up my question." I faced the owl. "Unless you'd like to let me use tomorrow's in advance?"

"I can't tell you who the killer is, you turnip," he said. "But I *can* tell you that if the guardian did as you suspected, I would have chased her out of the library myself."

He took flight, leaving me gaping after him. "Did he just…"

"Yes," said Cass. "You know, I almost believed you were right, too, but if Sylvester thought Jaxon *was* the killer, he wouldn't have let him stay here in the library."

"I guess not, but we already know Evangeline isn't infallible." The same went for the owl, however reluctant he might be to admit he had limits. "I'm going to trust that he's right, though. And I want to trust Grandma too."

Cass inclined her head. "Yes, and that boyfriend of yours is probably back by now. I thought I heard the door."

"I hope so." I led the way back to the stairs, and we climbed down. I half expected the guardian to appear and shove me into oblivion again, but she didn't have the same control over the library as Sylvester did. Good job, considering I might have made an enemy of her.

To my intense relief, Cass was right. Xavier waited in the lobby, next to an anxious-looking Estelle.

"Sorry I took so long." He swept over to meet me and drew me into a hug. "Your cousin told me everything."

"Good," I said distractedly. "I… Sorry. I just had a standoff with the guardian of the fourth-floor corridor."

"What?" Estelle frowned. "What brought that on?"

I took in a breath. "I thought the guardian of the fourth-floor corridor summoned Jaxon on purpose and sabotaged our attempts to cure Aunt Candace. Sylvester disagreed, and maybe I'm wildly off track, but the guardian led them to that pub. Laney saw it in Aunt Candace's thoughts."

"The corridor summoned up a fictional character to protect the library?" asked Estelle. "You know, it's plausible, but I wouldn't have thought even Grandma would go as far as to commit murder."

"It's not really her, is it?" I asked. "That's the problem. And the cure didn't work."

Estelle bit her lower lip. "Maybe I asked for the wrong thing. I'm sure the guardian *is* capable of powerful magic, but she can't have wanted everyone to target the library, can she?"

We both jumped when someone rapped on the door, but a glance out the window told me it was Laney. I opened the door, and Laney darted into the lobby.

"Sorry I startled you," she said. "I didn't know if you wanted me to come back in without knocking. I had to dodge around a mob to get back. They're seriously mad at Jaxon. Did he really find *another* body?"

"I don't know if he's the one who found her, but they think he killed Corrine as well as Patti and Olli," I said. "What did Evangeline have to say for herself?"

"Not a lot." She scowled. "She slithered back into her house before I caught up to her, and then that mob showed up."

"So, she didn't explain herself."

"No, but I think she was lying earlier."

"About what?" I asked. "You mean when she told everyone to come to her if they wanted to learn how to become a vampire?"

"Kind of," she said. "I didn't read her thoughts—I can't— but I got a sense that she was trying to lull everyone into a false sense of security so that the real killer assumed she wasn't on their tail."

"Then why did she send everyone after Jaxon on purpose?" I asked disbelievingly. "He *is* the killer, isn't he?"

"That's just it. I don't think he is."

"He has to be." There weren't any other contenders, were there? I caught sight of a pair of eyes staring at me from the tree. Or rather, glaring at me. "What, Sylvester?"

"What's he doing?" Estelle asked.

"Nothing much." I pointed at the tree. "He's lurking in there. He also pretty much said Jaxon isn't the killer, too, but he didn't offer any alternatives, and I'm still not convinced."

He'd had a point in that everything in the library was a creation of biblio-witch magic, though. Even Sylvester himself, perhaps. What kind of clue had he been trying to give me? That anything could become real, given a touch of our magic? How could that knowledge solve any of our current problems?

"He's usually right, isn't he?" Laney said. "And Evangeline is too. Much to my annoyance."

"There's only one way to find out," I said. "We need to speak to Evangeline ourselves. And this time, we'll make her listen to us."

14

The high street was almost deserted as Laney, Xavier, and I walked swiftly to the vampires' home. I didn't know where the mob had disappeared to, but if they'd been at the vampires' home, they weren't around now. When we reached the renovated church, Laney glided ahead of me and knocked on the door.

To my surprise, Evangeline answered this time. "Aurora, I'm surprised to see you walking around."

"I don't have a choice." I took in a breath. "You knew that as soon as you implied Jaxon was the killer, the mob would go after my family."

"I rather hoped otherwise," she said, "but your aunt and the vampire have escaped, have they not?"

"What of my other family members?" Anger choked the words in my throat. "Is Jaxon the killer or not?"

"If he isn't, a rogue is the only other option aside from your own people," Xavier put in. "You know that rogues have targeted Rory's family in the past and that she can't afford to overlook this."

"Also, three people are dead, and the only suspect has

probably left town." Unless Jaxon was still within Ivory Beach, of course. "If not him, then who?"

"That," she said, "is what I intend to find out, if you'll allow me to do so. Do trust that I have the situation in hand, Aurora."

And she closed the door. Perplexed, I turned to Laney. "Where does she think the killer is hiding?"

"Among the mob?" she suggested. "Maybe she plans to corner them alone."

"Or at the pub," I said. "There's nobody left there, though. Except maybe the guy at the bar…"

"Might be worth asking him some questions while the others aren't there," Laney said.

Since the pub was on the way downhill anyway, we halted outside, and Laney opened the door. When we entered, Shaw was alone behind the bar, and he looked startled to see us enter. "What… Oh, it's you."

"Did everyone else leave?" I walked closer to the bar, and he shifted uncomfortably on his feet.

"I can make you a cocktail, or…"

"No, thanks." The place was quiet without the karaoke club dominating the bar, and the back door still was slightly ajar. "Aren't the police here?"

"Not yet." He kept wiping down the counter without meeting my eyes. "Guess they're busy dealing with that lot."

The mob? Wasn't Aunt Adelaide at the police station? You'd think the dead body outside the pub would have been a priority, despite the mess the karaoke goers had left behind. Half-empty cocktail glasses had been discarded on every surface, and their strong smell filled the air. Fruit cocktails and something else. Something that reminded me of my potion-brewing lesson.

Out of the corner of my eye, I saw Laney move, darting behind the bar.

"What are you doing?" Shaw twisted around to her. "You're a vampire?"

"Not very quick on the uptake, are you?" Laney lifted a bottle into the air. "How many more people were you planning to poison?"

He gaped at her, panic flickering across his face. "What?"

"You." That was where I'd smelled it before. *Poison.* "You killed Corrine."

Why didn't I think of it before? Who else had been able to walk around the pub without anyone giving him a second glance?

He gave a forced laugh. "What are you talking about?"

"What else is here?" Laney peered behind the bar. "I don't know what any of these potions are, but I bet anyone who's an expert will have a field day with this."

"Potions." Suspicion stirred. "You were testing them on the karaoke goers?"

Shaw opened and closed his mouth, seemingly weighing the odds of taking on a Reaper, a vampire, and a biblio-witch all at once.

"And what's this?" Laney resurfaced again with another bottle in her hand, this one bright red. "Blood, right?"

He flushed. "Give that back."

"You wanted to become a vampire?" My mouth went dry. "If you drank their blood, it would have given you some of their powers."

Such as the strength enough to break someone's neck with his bare hands. And if he planned to join the vampires, there was only one group that might have made him the offer. *The Founders.* He must have been approached by them, back when they'd still been recruiting.

"You're the one who prevented me from getting any further," he said accusingly. "If not for you and Evangeline, I'd already be a full vampire."

"You were working with Carlos Verdant?" My mind spun back to the house I'd burned down and the lab we'd found nearby. "Did he teach you to brew those potions?"

"Among other things." He reached for his wand, and Laney grabbed him from behind. He squirmed, twisting to escape her grip, but she held tightly.

"Why?" I asked. "What did any of those people do to you?"

"They got impatient," he said. "Patti and Corrine got it into their heads that they could use the library to wish to become vampires."

My heart jolted. "And where did that rumour come from?"

He twisted out of her grip with more agility than should have been possible for a regular person. Unless, that was, the person had been drinking vampire blood.

As Shaw took off at a sprint, Laney followed, as did Xavier. Cursing my normal human speed, I ran out of the pub and skidded to a halt when I spied Evangeline approaching.

"You!" I gasped out. "You knew he was working for Carlos Verdant, didn't you? You knew he was in contact with the Founders."

"I knew someone in that pub was involved with him," she corrected. "Multiple someones, potentially."

"Shaw's dad." I swore. "Shaw Senior. Is he still in there?"

"I would assume not." Her eyes narrowed. "At a guess, he'll have left town as soon as he suspected he was in danger of exposure."

"And you wanted him to think he wasn't. That's why you made that public display." I'd messed up her plan, but if she'd confided in me in the first place, I wouldn't have needed to use guesswork. "And Jaxon... Did you ever suspect him at all?"

"I did not," she said, "but I was curious as to why the library decided to use that form to protect itself."

Wait. "Were you conspiring with the *guardian?*"

"Yes, she was." Aunt Candace marched over to Evangeline, her expression surprisingly clear—and absolutely livid. "Sorry to disappoint you, but I worked out your game, and I won't be manipulated by you a moment longer."

"You aren't under his spell." The cure. Had it worked after all? More to the point, Evangeline had *known* about the guardian? Had she been aware of the corridor all along?

"No." Aunt Candace glared at the vampire. "I can't believe you conspired behind my back with my own library."

"Now, there's no need to sound so accusing." The vampires' leader displayed a fanged smile. "Our intention was to protect the secrets of your home. Isn't that what your mother would have wanted?"

"Keep her out of this," Aunt Candace spluttered. "You should both be ashamed of yourselves."

I could tell this was going to escalate way out of our control if we weren't careful. I might be angry with Evangeline, but adding myself to her list of enemies would only backfire on us when the real foe was still at large.

"Laney's gone after Shaw," I told Evangeline. "And so has Xavier. Are you going to help them?"

"I doubt it," Aunt Candace said. "She doesn't pursue her enemies. She lets them come to her."

"Correct." Evangeline gave her a thin-lipped smile. "Do come and visit me when you've calmed down, will you?"

And she was gone, leaving nothing but a blurred impression on my eyelids.

"She…" I took a step after her then turned to my aunt instead. "Where's Jaxon? When did the spell break?"

"You knew he was putting a spell on me, did you?" she said.

"I tried to tell you," I said. "We asked for a cure from the room on the fourth floor, but it didn't work."

Though her change of mood was abrupt enough that I wondered if the guardian had changed her mind and undid the spell after all.

"Did you now?" She grunted. "Luckily, Jaxon knows he shouldn't bother me any longer."

"If he's still wandering around, it's a problem," I said. "Since, you know, there's a mob after him."

"Yes." She tutted. "We'll just have to deliver the real killer to the police ourselves, won't we?"

"They might be miles away," I pointed out. "Laney and Xavier should be able to corner Shaw, but his dad is out there too. I don't know where he is."

"I do," she said. "I spent long enough in that pub to hear that he has a house just outside of Ivory Beach. And I know the address."

"You do?"

"That's right," she said, a hint of satisfaction in her voice. "Well? Are you ready?"

15

As I pulled out my Biblio-Witch Inventory, Aunt Candace hovered close behind me, a furious glare on her face. I didn't envy whichever vampire we ran into first, whether they allied with the Founders or otherwise. Scanning the page, I reached for the word *find* and hesitated. "Are you sure about this? We might be walking into a trap."

"Absolutely." She pulled out her own Biblio-Witch Inventory. I was glad that the spell she'd been under hadn't bewitched her into leaving it behind. "We can handle them."

"All right." I tapped a fingertip to the word *find*, picturing Laney and Xavier in my mind's eye.

We both vanished, landing on a street just outside of the town. Laney was already ahead of us, chasing Shaw at speed. He moved fast for someone who wasn't a full vampire yet, staying just out of her reach, and I didn't see any signs of Xavier. Where was he?

Aunt Candace lifted her wand. A bang rent the air like a firework, and Shaw flew several feet into the air. As he fell,

Laney reached out and caught him, pinning his arms behind his back.

"Gotcha." She grinned at us. "Thanks for the help. Oh, good, your aunt's finally free from that spell."

"Where's Xavier?" I hurried over to her.

"He was right behind me." She adjusted her grip on Shaw, who struggled against her hold. "You aren't a full vampire yet. You'll have to try harder than that."

"You're a traitor," he said, squirming. "They'll have your head for this."

"The Founders, right?" she said. "Let them try. Last I saw, they were locked in Evangeline's dungeon."

"Not all of them." A man walked into view, resembling a larger, older version of Shaw with fewer piercings. He moved with the swift, eerie grace that only one type of creature possessed.

This must be Shaw Senior. And he was already a full vampire.

He smiled, exposing pointed teeth. "Aurora, is it? And Candace too. I've heard a lot about both of you from my son."

"Why did you and your son kill those people?" I looked between them. "They didn't cause any harm."

"They asked too many questions," said Shaw Senior. "And risked our exposure. We worked hard to hide our activities from the other vampires and from the Reapers too."

"You worked hand in hand with Carlos Verdant." I felt sick. "You know he experimented on humans, don't you?"

He did, and he'd willingly offered himself up as a lab rat.

"You did the same, didn't you?" Aunt Candace put in. "Those cocktails. I knew there was a reason Jaxon told me not to drink them."

She hadn't? Jaxon had tried to help her? How much had he known? It wasn't like I could ask, and for all I knew, he was miles away, if he hadn't vanished outright when he'd ventured too far from the library.

"Now we're on the same page," said Shaw Senior, "I'll ask your vampire friend to let my son go, or else I'll have to see if any of my potions have an effect on Reapers."

"Xavier." My heart plunged. "Where is he?"

"His house." Laney lifted her head, still holding Shaw down. "I saw it in his mind. It's just… that way."

As she pointed down the street, Shaw wriggled out from underneath her and ran to join his father. The two of them—one vampire, one halfway there—didn't outnumber our group, but I didn't dare risk Xavier's safety. *They can't harm a Reaper. Can they?*

"Nice try." Laney bared her teeth at them. "I've been a vampire longer than you, I'm betting, and your son isn't one at all."

"I have other advantages," said Shaw Senior.

He ran at Laney. They both moved so fast that I didn't see anything until he had Laney held off the ground, his arm around her throat.

"Laney!" I lifted my wand and cast one of my go-to spells for vampires—a lullaby charm—but he dodged, and the spell shot straight past him. Laney choked, struggling against his grip.

Is that how he killed Patti?

A shadow fell over them both from behind, becoming the looming form of the guardian. Shaw's eyes bulged, and even his father stopped to stare at the newcomer.

"What are you?" he snarled.

"The guardian of the library." I seized on his distraction to cast another lullaby charm, and this one hit its mark. Shaw slumped instantly, but my second spell had no effect on his father.

"I think he's been drinking enhancement potions." Laney slipped out from his grasp, massaging her throat.

Shaw didn't try to grab her again. He crouched, scooped up his son's unconscious body, and fled from the guardian.

I took off in pursuit, Laney and Aunt Candace close behind me. The guardian followed, too, but I still didn't entirely trust it to fight on our side, nor was I clear on what it could actually do in a situation like this. Aside from messing with people's memories, it had never used magic outside of the library that I'd seen. Maybe it couldn't, and that was why it had conjured up Jaxon to help instead.

As we veered around a corner, Shaw Senior disappeared through the door of a detached redbrick house, closing the door behind him. Laney approached the door, still rubbing her neck with one hand.

"Careful," I warned. "We don't know what other tricks he might be hiding."

"I can handle him." Aunt Candace pointed her wand at the door and blew it clean off its hinges.

Inside the hall, the vampire spun to face us, standing in front of a half-open door. I didn't see any signs of Xavier, but he must be in here somewhere. As I ran forward, the vampire lifted a hand and flung a glass bottle towards us. I jumped back, and the glass smashed on the pavement, causing a plume of bright-red smoke to rise into the air. I stumbled, coughing, my vision turning red too.

Consciousness blinked out but only for a few seconds. When I opened my eyes, I lay on my back on carpeted floor. Nearby sat a table covered in an array of potions, and Aunt Candace lay on my right-hand side in a similar state of unconsciousness. On my left was Laney, and behind...

"Xavier?" I coughed, my mouth tasting foul from the potion's effects. He lay upon a long table, one arm drooping over the side. "Xavier!"

What did the vampire do to him?

"Don't waste your breath," said Shaw Senior. "This could have all been avoided, you know. But I won't forgive anyone who hurts my son."

"You *killed* three people." In the corner of the room hovered the guardian, but I had a sinking suspicion I'd been right in that her abilities were limited outside of the library.

"That creature is a nuisance." He followed my gaze. "It doesn't seem to have strong magic, but I did wonder why the pub's visitors kept forgetting everything Shaw told them. Is it another creation of your library's?"

"Another creation?"

He knew what Jaxon was, and in the absence of any other options, he—or the Founders—must have been the source of the rumours. The thought that any of them knew what the library was truly capable of sent a wave of pure horror crashing over me.

"Yes, the man who turned me had some interesting stories to tell." He gave a smile. "Yes, you aren't as good at keeping secrets as you might think. Your grandmother had quite the reputation."

Grandma. "You're lying."

Carlos Verdant hadn't met Grandma, had he?

"Oh, it wasn't him." His smile widened. "You might have had some practise at hiding your thoughts but not enough. You're an open book, Aurora, and so is your library."

"He didn't turn you." A second wave of horror crested. "Then… Mortimer Vale."

The door slammed open, and Jaxon ran in. A hiss slipped between his teeth as he faced the other vampire. Scrambling to my feet, I spied my wand lying on a nearby table and edged closer.

Aunt Candace stirred, and her gaze immediately went to Jaxon. "You can't fool me again, Jaxon. It's over."

"Not the time," I said out of the corner of my mouth.

Jaxon and Shaw Senior collided, crashing through the open door and into the hall. Hoping Jaxon had the upper hand, I shook Laney's shoulder. It was Xavier who really had me worried. He lay still—too still—in a way I'd never seen before.

"Candace." Jaxon was back, his clothes and hair dishevelled. "I didn't intend to deceive you."

"Is Shaw Senior…" I trailed off when the door opened wider, and Evangeline came sailing into the room.

"You"—Aunt Candace went bright red, spluttering—"planned to show up all along, did you?"

"It's what she does." I gave Laney another shake, and then moved to Xavier. "He knocked him out. How can he have knocked out a Reaper?"

"That is not a question I can answer, Aurora." She gestured behind herself to Shaw Senior, who lay in a groaning heap. "However, I can take care of this little problem."

She lifted the new vampire with ease, and they both vanished through the front door.

"Ow, my head." Laney pushed to her knees. "Did I hear Evangeline?"

"Are you okay?" I shook Xavier's shoulder, my heart racing. "Xavier. He won't wake up."

"Oh no." Laney scanned the room. "There's bound to be a cure somewhere in here, right?"

"I wouldn't count on it." Panic spiked as the memory of her coma and all its surrounding stress came soaring back. "The Founders don't tend to worry as much about that part."

"No." She picked up a bottle then another. "I don't know what any of these do."

I looked for my aunt, but she had eyes only for Jaxon. "How much did you know?" she demanded of him. "Did you try to manipulate me from the start? Was all that nonsense about not knowing anything about this world for show?"

"No," he said. "I *was* confused when I first came here. It was only when I met the vampires' leader that I realised what was going on."

"And I was just a convenient tool, was I?"

I tuned out their argument, examining the rows of bottles, but my potion-making lessons hadn't been this advanced, and most of these were new creations of Shaw and his father. As shadows rustled along the floor, I lifted my head to address the guardian. "Can you help cure him? Please?"

No answer. Tears burned my eyes.

"I'm sorry I accused you," I whispered. "I didn't know, and you *were* prepared to go to extreme lengths to protect the library. But if Xavier doesn't wake up…" If nothing else, the Grim Reaper would ensure my whole family paid the price for it.

The guardian moved in a motion that mimicked someone lifting a hand. Beckoning, perhaps, or asking me to trust her.

I had no choice. I had to trust the guardian—and the library—to help me fix this.

16

Evangeline returned with more vampires in tow to take apart the homemade lab and retrieve the unconscious Shaw, and Laney carried Xavier back to the library while my aunt and I used transportation spells. Jaxon and the guardian were left behind, but they could make their own way back as swiftly as the vampires could.

"Rory." Estelle let out a gasp when we landed in the lobby. "Oh, Aunt Candace. Laney said you caught the killer?"

"Shaw the bartender," I said. "And his dad. Is your mum still at the police station?"

"She is, but… The *bartender* was the killer?"

"His dad worked for the Founders," I explained. "He was brewing potions, including… including ones that worked on Reapers."

She sucked in a breath. "Xavier. What's wrong with him?"

"I don't know." I crouched beside his prone body, tears leaking from my eyes. "I'm going to have to ask the fourth-floor corridor, but I wouldn't be surprised if the guardian refused to help me."

"I'm sure she will," said Laney. "Oh, there's Jaxon."

Aunt Candace narrowed her eyes at the window, where the vampire stood beside the hovering form of the guardian. "We're not letting him back in here."

"I thought you wanted to get rid of him," I said. "Though you might be able to banish him without inviting him into the library, now you actually want him gone."

"When did the spell wear off?" asked Estelle. "I thought the cure didn't work."

"The guardian," I explained. "Hence why I'm not sure she'll help. She was using both of them to lure out whoever was working with the Founders."

"And where's Evangeline in all this?" Cass stepped out from behind the shelves. "Did she ever answer your questions?"

"Yeah, and she did eventually show up and help," I said. "She took Shaw Senior—Shaw's dad—and she'll probably lock him in her dungeon with the other captives. He'd turned full vampire, and his son was planning to do the same."

"Shaw Senior." She snorted. "That's a terrible name for a vampire."

"I agree." Aunt Candace glowered at Jaxon on the other side of the window. Aunt Candace muttered curses under her breath. "If you ask me, I should send him somewhere far worse than back into his story. Into one of my horror novels, perhaps."

"Write him into the next one," I suggested. "I don't think he was trying to deceive you. The guardian, though…"

"She and I are no longer friends."

"We still need to go to the fourth floor." I beckoned to Aunt Candace. "It's up to you if you want to bring him with you. You might be able to use your Biblio-Witch Inventory to banish him without him coming in."

"No." She took in a breath. "I shall give him a piece of my mind on the way upstairs."

"I'll wait for my mum down here," Estelle said. "Rory, I'm sure Xavier will be fine."

I hope so. Laney carried Xavier upstairs ahead of me, and I picked up the pace to stay out of hearing distance of Aunt Candace's furious whispered argument with Jaxon. The guardian overtook all of us with ease, her cloak-like form rippling behind, and I found myself wondering if this was the first time she'd gone to meet with Evangeline or just the first that we'd been aware of. How far back did they go?

When we reached the fourth floor, we let Aunt Candace and Jaxon approach the door first. The vampire was uncharacteristically subdued, and Aunt Candace gave him one last searching look before she lifted her pen and wrote her wish on the door.

I hung back to give them some privacy and sensed the guardian hovering behind me, an unspeaking presence.

"Why?" I whispered to the creature. "Why make an alliance with Evangeline? I thought you wanted to avoid exposing yourself to the vampires."

No response came from the guardian, but I hadn't expected one. When the door closed on Jaxon, Aunt Candace stalked past us without a word. Sensing she wanted to be left alone, I turned to the room myself, my chest tightening.

I pressed the tip of my pen to the door and wrote, *I wish for a cure to wake up Xavier.*

The door swung inward. Hardly breathing, I entered the small room, which had the same layout as it had when I'd retrieved the cure for Laney's coma—down to the phoenix feather.

"The cure is the same?" The potion must be a variation of the poison the Founders had used on Laney, except adapted for Reapers instead of vampires.

I picked up the feather from the table and returned to the corridor. Laney had placed Xavier on his back, and the guardian hovered behind. I held the feather over him, and its glow brightened to gold.

As it fluttered from my grip, a familiar glow spread across Xavier's skin, almost too bright to look at. For a heartbeat, nothing happened. Then he stirred, his eyes opening.

"Xavier." I gasped and threw my arms around him. He hugged me back, and for a moment, there was nothing but the two of us.

Gradually, other voices filtered in. Cass was talking to Laney and Aunt Candace, and it was so incongruous to see the three of them getting along that I reluctantly let go of Xavier and addressed my cousin. "Cass, did you want to make a wish too?"

"Hell, no."

"What wish?" asked Laney.

I rubbed my eyes on the back of my hand. "I don't know. Answers, maybe. I want to know how long Evangeline has known about this place."

"You think the room will tell you that?" Cass asked skeptically. "Why not ask Evangeline herself?"

"She hasn't exactly proven herself to be the paragon of truth lately."

"You're all still in here?" Estelle came upstairs and peered into the corridor. "Rory… Oh, good, he's awake."

"He is." I squeezed Xavier's hand, a fresh wave of relief seeping through me. "And Jaxon's gone. Is your mum back?"

"Yes, and she wants to hear what's going on."

"I bet."

I told Xavier everything, too, as we climbed down from the fourth floor and then continued down three flights of stairs to the lobby. He'd only missed the final standoff with Shaw and his father and Jaxon and the guardian's unexpected intervention, so it didn't take too long for him to catch up. I also spied

Sylvester peering out of the tree on the way down, but he didn't announce his presence openly. Had *he* known of Evangeline's friendship with the guardian—and with Grandma? Somehow, I doubted it, and while his mistrust of the guardian had been justified, neither of us would have ever guessed the real reason.

Downstairs, we found none other than Evangeline in the lobby, speaking to Aunt Adelaide.

"I thought you were busy with your new prisoners," I said to the vampires' leader. "Why are you here?"

To apologise, I hoped, but given the dangerous glare on Aunt Candace's face, no apology would be enough.

"I simply wanted to offer your aunt an explanation," she said. "I'm glad those rowdy humans didn't do any harm."

"What? The mob?"

"They showed up at the police station," Aunt Adelaide explained.

"That's where they went?" I asked, alarmed. "Did Edwin have to lock any of them up?"

"No, but he came close." Aunt Adelaide nodded to Evangeline. "Luckily, they calmed down when one of her people brought in that bartender."

"Shaw's in the humans' prison?"

"He is," said Evangeline. "I thought that would be more appropriate."

"Are you going to tell us the truth now?" Aunt Candace asked. "How long did you know Jaxon?"

"Not as long as you think," she said. "I've spent the past few weeks looking for Carlos Verdant's allies and the remnants of his schemes to target mortals and make potions to manipulate others. That is a shared goal between myself and your grandmother, Aurora."

"The guardian isn't our grandma." She was an echo, nothing more. "You knew Grandma, too, didn't you?"

"You did." Estelle stared at her too. "Grandma was friends with the vampires?"

"I highly doubt they were friends." Aunt Adelaide's mouth thinned. "Whatever the case, this is not your first encounter with the guardian, is it?"

No, which means she already knew about the corridor. No wonder Jaxon hadn't thought of her as a threat, but her words brought back the reminder that Carlos Verdant wasn't the one who'd turned Shaw.

"No." I spoke quickly. "It isn't, and... and Shaw said Mortimer Vale is the one who turned him. He knows too. About the guardian and everything else."

"I think I shall leave you to discuss this amongst yourselves." Evangeline offered a smile, her attention lingering on me for a moment. "Good night."

As she vanished through the front door, Aunt Candace made to follow her. Aunt Adelaide caught her arm. "I wouldn't."

"That manipulator," she fumed. "Conspiring behind our backs. I don't believe for a minute that our mother would ever have confided in her."

I didn't want to believe it either. I'd gone to such lengths to keep the journal from Evangeline that I'd never considered she might have been close to any of my family members after all. "She might not have. Mortimer Vale knew her, too, and *they* certainly weren't friends."

"He can't have known," Aunt Adelaide said. "It's not possible."

"Maybe not everything, but he did know about the corridor, at the very least," I said. "I think he and Grandma might have been acquainted." *Like Dad.* How far back did the Founders' link to my family truly go?

"The good news is that none of us is going to be arrested for murder," Cass said. "Don't forget that part."

"That's correct." Sylvester fluttered over to land on the desk. "And one of you has a birthday in a week."

"Rory. Right, I forgot," Estelle said apologetically.

"So did I," I reassured her. "I don't want to make a big deal of it. We had other priorities."

"You don't now," said the owl.

"I know that." I gave him an eye roll. "Also, I take it you knew the guardian wasn't our enemy? Not our *real* enemy," I amended when Aunt Candace scoffed.

"Obviously," he said. "That guardian and I might not be friends, but we do have some level of understanding."

"Did you know she was allied with Evangeline?"

"No, but I rather think it'll be a weight off your mind not to have to hide the corridor's existence from her. Am I correct?"

"She's still much too interested in my dad's journal." That wasn't connected to Grandma, though. While my dad had worked with her to make the Spell Assistant, among other things, his misadventures in search of rare books and his entanglements with the Founders had occurred without the rest of my family members being involved. Her supposed friendship with Grandma, if it had existed, was much earlier. Given that Evangeline was likely centuries old, I'd somehow never considered that she might have befriended older family members of mine, even before the library's creation.

"She is," said Estelle. "Strange that she never told us she knew about the corridor sooner."

"I imagine she found it amusing to watch us go out of our way to avoid mentioning it," said Cass.

"She's too fond of mind games," Aunt Adelaide said. "Whatever her relationship to my mother, I doubt I'll ever consider her a friend."

"Nor me," I said. "The mob has gone home, then? There's no danger of any of them showing up here?"

"No," she replied. "Like I said, they left the jail. I believe some went to the pub and were disappointed to find no staff waiting to serve them drinks."

"Pity for them," said Aunt Candace. "Personally, I shall never set foot in that place again."

"Nobody will, considering its owners are in jail," I remarked, leaning closer to Xavier. I didn't want to let him out of my sight, though I knew he'd have to report back to his boss sooner or later, and it wasn't going to be pretty.

He wrapped an arm around me from behind and murmured, "I'm fine, Rory. Don't worry. The potion didn't hurt me."

I twisted on the spot, peering up at his face. "Are you going to tell your boss?"

"I should, but he's not going to take it well."

"That's what I thought." If the Founders were developing ways to subdue even the Reapers, the Grim Reaper would be furious.

"But I'll tell him later." He drew me closer. "We're long overdue a date."

"Agreed." And we would stay here in the library, beneath the Christmas tree's glittering lights. By the week's end, the place would be kitted out, ready for the season, and all of this would be behind us.

The night might be dark, but dawn always followed, and unlike the vampires, I'd be awake to see the sunrise.

ABOUT THE AUTHOR

Elle Adams lives in the middle of England, where she spends most of her time reading an ever-growing mountain of books, planning her next adventure, or writing. Elle's books are humorous mysteries with a paranormal twist, packed with magical mayhem.

She also writes urban and contemporary fantasy novels as Emma L. Adams.

Find Elle on Facebook at https://www.facebook.com/pg/ElleAdamsAuthor/

www.ingramcontent.com/pod-product-compliance
Lightning Source LLC
Chambersburg PA
CBHW061446210726
48287CB00007B/2383